"So...will you put on your cowboy duds for me?"

Meg reached to stroke Clint's cheek.

"But you said you wouldn't know what to do with a real cowboy." He brought her hand to his mouth and placed a string of kisses there.

"I didn't think I did." Her voice grew husky. "But you've changed my mind."

He looked into her eyes, and desire hit him hard. "I didn't think I'd know what to do with a TV star, either."

"But you do. Trust me, you do."

Clint wanted her so much, he had to fight not to grab her. He stood up suddenly. "Had enough of this dinner for a while?"

"If that's an invitation to visit your bedroom, I accept."

His heart beat loud and fast. "It was a solid-gold, engraved invitation."

Meg got out of her chair and held out her hand. "Then let's go get it on, cowboy."

Dear Reader,

Eighteen months ago my career got a huge boost from the "Reading with Ripa" Book Club. But before Kelly Ripa, I was first and foremost a Harlequin Temptation author. My first published book in 1984 was a Temptation novel, and for years I dreamed of writing Harlequin Temptation's 1000th book. This is that book.

Harlequin Temptation has grown, changed, evolved. And so have I. We're still together after all these years. It seemed fitting to set this book in my home state of Arizona, and to give it a cowboy hero in tribute to all the cowboy heroes I've created and loved. But the heroine is a TV talk-show host from New York. You don't have to look far to find my inspiration for that character!

It's with great pleasure that I give you this book. It stands on the shoulders of 999 other terrific reads. I'm honored to be here.

Fondly,

Vicki Lewis Thompson

Books by Vicki Lewis Thompson

VICKI LEWIS THOMPSON

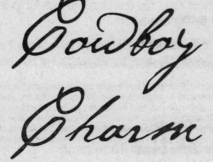

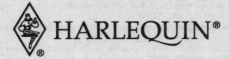

HARLEQUIN®

TORONTO • NEW YORK • LONDON
AMSTERDAM • PARIS • SYDNEY • HAMBURG
STOCKHOLM • ATHENS • TOKYO • MILAN • MADRID
PRAGUE • WARSAW • BUDAPEST • AUCKLAND

To all the fabulous Temptresses, past, present and future.
You've made Temptation what it is today,
and I couldn't be in better company.

ISBN 0-373-69200-5

KILLER COWBOY CHARM

www.eHarlequin.com

Printed in U.S.A.

1

"HERE THEY ARE, your *Meg and Mel in the Morning* co-hosts, Meg Delancy and Mel Harrison!"

Beaming at the wildly applauding studio audience, Meg bounced onto the set followed by a suave and smiling Mel. Meg had to act as if she hadn't seen the ratings and didn't know their number-one rank was in danger.

Nobody seemed to know why, either.

But rumors flew, including the one implying that the chemistry wasn't right between her and Mel. If a studio exec believed that for a minute, Meg would be the one to go. Mel had established the show eight years ago and nobody would be looking to replace silver-haired Mel Harrison.

She would not lose this job.

At a tender age, sitting spellbound by Captain Kangaroo and Mr. Rogers, she'd announced that someday she'd have her own television show. Her parents had laughed.

When she'd insisted on turning their Brooklyn living room into a studio and interviewing the neighbors in front of whatever audience she could drag in, her family had thought it was cute. But they'd never taken her seriously.

As she'd persisted in her goal through high school and even college, their indulgence had turned to alarm. Nobody they knew had ever succeeded in the entertainment field. They predicted she'd fail and suggested nursing, teaching, banking, anything but her crazy notion. Even her best friends had advised her to try something less ambitious. At their warnings, she'd become even more determined.

Then she'd landed a gofer job on what was then *Marnie and Mel in the Morning*. Working tirelessly, she'd eventually made it to the tech crew, but she considered it only a step on her way to the co-host chair. Marnie's emergency appendectomy gave Meg a chance to substitute for the star, and Marnie's decision to leave the show for a role in a feature film left the spot open. Meg convinced Mel to give it to her.

Her family and friends still didn't quite believe it. Meg knew they expected her newfound fame to evaporate any minute. She'd be damned if she'd let that happen.

As the applause from the studio audience continued, pumped up off-camera by executive producer Sharon Dempsey, Meg and Mel settled into their cushy seats and picked up the mugs waiting for them on the low coffee table.

Mel took a sip from his mug of water colored to look like coffee and turned to Meg. "Great weekend in Manhattan, huh?" he said. By custom, he usually had the opening line of the show. "Halloween parties galore, and it was actually warm for a change. Here it is November first, and no snow. So, did you have a good weekend?"

"Friday night I went out with my girlfriends, but the fish weren't biting, if you know what I mean."

"Too bad. What about Saturday?"

"I watched my DVD of *The Mummy*. Alone." She took a swallow of her watered-down diet cola, pretending to savor something that tasted like mouthwash. Her lack of a social life was a running gag on the show, but she was getting sick of it. She had no one to blame but herself, though. Focusing on this job had left no time for cultivating a relationship.

"I thought you watched that movie last weekend."

"So I have a crush on Brendan Fraser." But she would rather have spent the night with a guy who wasn't an image on her TV screen. Ironically, now that she'd reached her goal, she'd discovered that being Mel's co-host came with certain restrictions.

Despite the sexual banter they occasionally shared on the show, Mel was a conservative guy. A torrid affair that scorched the pages of *The Enquirer* could get her fired. To keep her girl-next-door image, she'd have to zoom from first date to safely married.

In truth, she didn't want to marry anyone until she'd established herself as a TV personality, which could take several years. Only then might she be in the market. A husband and kids would be nice—*if* she could juggle a family and work. A husband would have to know going in that she wasn't giving up her career.

Mel clucked his tongue and looked fatherly. "I don't know what's wrong with the eligible bachelors around here. A gorgeous redhead like you, they should be lined up outside your apartment door."

"Maybe all the good ones are taken. I'm guessing you went to a Halloween party?" In contrast to Meg with her nonexistent social life, Mel and his wife never seemed to stay home.

"Evie and I went to a great costume party at the Starlight Room. And I have to tell you, the hit of the night was a guy who came as a cowboy, all duded up. He even did rope tricks. The women swooned."

Meg put a hand to her heart and sighed. "I *love* cowboys, especially when they wear those tight jeans that show off their terrific…personalities." She waggled her eyebrows and the audience laughed.

In truth she did have a real crush on cowboy types. Her dad had tuned in everything Western on TV, from reruns of *Gunsmoke* to all the Clint Eastwood spaghetti Westerns, and with only one TV set in the house, she'd watched with him. The heroes had seemed exotic and so removed from her life that they'd become a secret fantasy.

"Unfortunately, turns out this cowboy was gay."

"You see? See what I mean? Taken or gay. At least that's the way it seems in New York." Meg decided to ad-lib. "Maybe I need to go out West and find myself a rope-twirling, spur-jingling, heterosexual-to-the-core cowboy."

Mel shook his perfectly coifed head. "No such thing anymore. That's all Hollywood stuff."

"I don't believe it. I'll bet the West is still chock-full of sexy cowboys, swaggering around in snug denim with their thumbs hooked through their belt loops. Yum."

"I'm afraid that dream cowboy is a myth," Mel said. "But speaking of myths and cowboys, we have the perfect guest today. *Lord of the Rings* and *Hidalgo* star Viggo Mortensen is here to talk about his next project. Now there's a fantasy cowboy for you, Meg. I assume you saw Viggo in *Hidalgo*?"

"Six times."

"Thought so. We also have Snoop Dogg paying us a long-overdue visit, plus we've discovered a magician who's performing street shows all over town. If you haven't seen him yet, he'll truly astound you. We'll be back, right after this."

The moment the commercial break started, Sharon hurried over clutching her earphones to her head as if she couldn't believe the info coming through them. "You guys, the phones are lighting up! Everyone wants to see Meg go out West and look for her cowboy!"

Meg laughed. "Oh, sure, that's gonna happen. It was just a joke. I've never been out West, and I have no intention of—"

"Think again," Sharon said. "We need a shot in the arm, and this could be it!"

"You know, it's not a bad idea," Mel said. "Not bad at all."

"It's a great idea!" Sharon glowed with excitement. "How about this—we call it the search for the Hottest Cowboy in the West."

Mel nodded. "I like it already."

Meg wasn't liking it at all. Leaving the studio was a bad idea. Temporary replacements could become permanent fixtures if you left. "I don't know about this, Sharon. I think we should consider it more carefully."

"We'll iron out the details when we have more time, but I'm getting goose bumps, which means this is a dynamite concept. I can see you going remote with Jamie. You'll find candidates, and then we bring them on the show and the audience votes for the winner. We'll have a big cash prize and tons of promo. Is that awesome, or what?"

Meg didn't hear much besides the phrase *going remote*. "But I can't leave the show to run around looking for cowboys."

"Sure you can," Mel said. "For a few days. Shar's right. This could be exactly what we need to boost the ratings."

"But who would you get to co-host while I'm gone?" But she already knew. Mona Swift. She'd been the runner-up for the job a year ago, and she was hovering like a vulture waiting for Meg to fail. Mona even had the right first initial to slide right into the co-host's chair. Before Meg could blink, it would be *Mona and Mel in the Morning*.

"We'd get Mona," Shar said. "I'm sure she'd be happy to fill in for a little while."

No kidding. She'd be shickled titless to take my job away permanently. "Listen, this will cost way too much money. Food, lodging—"

"No, it won't," Mel said. "We'll get ranches to donate space to hold the competition. If we set it up alphabetically, we could even start with George's ranch in Arizona. He'd love the publicity."

Meg made one last appeal, focusing desperately on Mel. "It'll really shake up the routine. You know how you hate change."

"Yeah, I hate change, but I hate sagging ratings worse. The fact is, I agree totally with Sharon on this. You need to go out there, Meg."

And that, Meg knew, was the end of that. Mel had spoken.

"ME AND MY big freakin' mouth!" Meg stared out the window of the communications van she and Jamie had rented from an affiliate in Phoenix. They were now somewhere south of Tucson, going to George's ranch. George, multimillionaire and poker buddy of Mel, had bought the place as an investment and was sitting on it waiting for prices to go up. He rarely visited. Meg could understand why.

Jamie sighed and shook his head. "Are you gonna bitch for the entire two weeks? Because I can match you bitch for bitch. Alison and I are in a very tricky stage of our relationship. Anything could happen while I'm gone."

"I know, I know. But which is more important, Alison

giving in to the temptation to date somebody else, or Mona taking permanent possession of my co-host chair? I mean, you could make a play to get Alison back. I'm *sure* you could get Alison back." She thought Jamie, short and wiry, was perfect for Alison, who was short and plump. They both had the same kind of curly dark hair and they'd produce adorable children someday.

"Thanks for assuming I'll have to try and get her back. Thanks a hell of a lot. And for the record, I don't think Mona can steal your job. You have a solid fan base. Besides, I predict the camera's going to pick up on her insincerity. You've made it because you're sincere."

"Correction, I haven't made it. Ratings are down. But I can tell you that I sincerely hate being here." She waved a hand at the scenery. "Will you look at this countryside? There is *nothing* out here. No Bloomie's, no Saks. Just mountains, hills and windmills."

"Cowboy country."

"Will you stop saying that? I like my cowboys in the middle of Madison Square Garden, not in the middle of nowhere. I'm never ad-libbing on the show again. Never. It was supposed to be a joke—me, the ultimate city girl, combing the boonies for a date."

"It *is* a joke. That's why it's such a great idea. I just wish they'd assigned Dave or Wayne to this gig instead of me."

Meg glanced at him, taking pity on the poor guy. "For what it's worth, I'm glad they sent you. I don't get along with Dave or Wayne anything like I do with you."

"Hey, you're all right, too, but I'm at risk of losing Alison while we trot around God's country. Sharon might have fired me if I'd refused, though, so here I am."

"Yeah, where are we, anyway?" Meg picked up the map from the floor of the van.

"We're coming up on the bustling metropolis of Son-oita."

"Where is it?" Meg squinted through the windshield as the late-afternoon sun cast a melon-colored glow over a crossroads with no stoplight. "There're, like, five or six buildings at this intersection."

"Behold Sonoita."

"You're kidding, right? There's more to it down the road."

"I don't think so, Meg. This looks about the way they described it to me in Phoenix. At the intersection we go left about two miles, hang a right, and we'll be at the Circle W."

Meg let out a wail. "There's no downtown! There's not even a mall! Where am I supposed to get my lattes? I'm on the damned set of *Gunsmoke*!"

Jamie grinned. "Wish I had that on tape. The viewers would love it."

Meg blew out a breath and flopped back against the seat. "The viewers are so not going to have the satisfaction of seeing me whine, Jamie Cranston, so forget about it." She laid her head back. "But I would kill for a steaming mochaccino right now."

"You never know. They might have all the amenities at the Circle W."

Meg stared bleakly at the rolling brown hills. She'd seen enough Westerns on TV to know that was highly unlikely. "Don't bet on it, Jamie, my boy. Don't bet on it."

CLINT HAD HOPED some hard labor followed by a hot shower would improve his mood, but he was still pissed. George Forester might own the Circle W now. He might pay Clint's salary, plus the salaries of the other hands. But he had no right to turn the historic ranch into a media playground.

Good thing that Clint's dad hadn't lived to see this. And as for Clint's great-grandfather, a self-made man who'd built the ranch from nothing to what had once been the finest spread in Sonoita—Clint didn't even want to imagine what Clemson Walker would have had to say about this television stunt.

Clint didn't have the power to stop it, but he planned to stay the hell out of the limelight. A little voice in his head kept whispering that there was a cash prize involved, and Clint needed cash if he ever expected to buy back the ranch. Then he'd think of what he'd have to do for a chance at that cash and his blood would run cold.

He'd received a letter outlining the whole procedure. Meg Delancy and her cameraman would visit seven Western states, beginning alphabetically with Arizona. Using a local ranch as a base, Meg would hold a competition open to any cowboy living in the state. She'd watch them rope and ride first and conduct personal interviews afterward. Three finalists from each state would appear on TV in New York, where the viewers would choose the winner.

Yeah, the cash prize would be a help to him, but it wouldn't be enough to buy back the ranch. Considering that he'd have to parade himself in front of a TV camera in order to have a chance to win, the money didn't seem nearly enough. Some guys said the prize would be only the beginning, that the winner would be able to parlay the TV appearance into something more, like commercials.

That concept really gave Clint the shakes. He'd rather ride a killer bull than speak lines in front of a television camera. Even worse would be carrying around the designation of Hottest Cowboy in the West. He'd die of embarrassment.

No, he'd have to stick to his current program and hope that Gabriel would finish in the money next year. Clint had scraped together the funds to buy him, believing the promising quarterhorse could eventually make him enough to buy back the Circle W. The plan would take time, because the amount needed was large, but it could work, especially if George grew tired of sitting on his investment.

Gabriel would run his first race in three months. This TV business would interfere with Gabriel's training, which was another reason Clint resented the intrusion. He wanted nothing to do with the whole mess.

Yet he was worried he might somehow be dragged into it. Several of his neighbors had asked if he was competing, as if they expected him to. A couple of women had winked and said he'd be a natural. That made him wonder if Meg would put pressure on him and imply he was being a poor sport for staying out of it. He wanted to eliminate any chance of that.

Then, while mucking out stalls this morning, he'd had an inspiration. He'd play dumb, pretend he knew nothing about running a ranch and say his sixty-year-old foreman Tucker Benson was the expert. Tuck could take the heat and cater to this city woman's whims.

Once Clint had been informed that the Arizona segment of the search would be held at the Circle W, which meant he would be housing Meg for two nights, he'd taken a look at the show. He'd sat there shaking his head at that smiling, silly woman who would soon be invading his precious ranch. She'd be more out of place than an eyelash curler on a trail ride.

Clint was vaguely familiar with eyelash curlers and all the other appliances that women used to improve on nature. He didn't begrudge them those toys, but he became a little cranky if the primping got in the way of living. More than not, it seemed to. He was still looking for a woman who'd climb out of bed and join him for a breakfast ride without spending twenty minutes fixing her face.

His brief stint watching "Meg and Mel in the Morning" had convinced him that the woman coming to the Circle W was as far from his ideal as a person could get. So why had he showered in preparation for her arrival? Oh, yeah. To wash off the smell of manure, so she would think he was a greenhorn who didn't even know how to sit a horse, let alone muck out a stall. Certainly not the ultimate cowboy.

As the plan gelled in his mind, he searched his closet and came up with a pair of pleated slacks he hadn't worn since his dad's funeral. He looked like a dude in those slacks, plus they had a really sad association tacked onto them. But wearing them might be just the trick, along with the narrow leather belt he'd bought to go with the outfit.

In fact, he should put on a dress shirt, too. And loafers. The loafers were buried under a pile of boots, but at last he located them. The loafers had been around for ten years, at least, because he'd had them in college. Looked like he'd be wearing them for the next two days. Finally, for good measure, he slicked back his dark hair.

The invasion could come at any minute, so he went in search of Tuck. He found the weathered foreman down by the round pen putting Gabriel through his paces. Tuck was a hell of a trainer, and if anyone could get Gabriel ready, this was the guy. Clint had known him all his life.

Tuck had been a good cowman in his day, too, but the Circle W had stopped running cattle several years ago. Clint's dad had been mired in debt by the time he'd sold to George Forester, and the cash from the sale had all gone to pay off those debts. Now the ranch's income came from boarding and training horses for all the folks who'd moved to the area recently. The Circle W also offered trail rides and cookouts for the tourists, and every year there were more tourists showing up in Sonoita.

In the beginning of his association with George, Clint had tried to interest him in quarterhorse racing, but George only cared about land values, so Clint had decided to pursue the racing angle on his own. He was lucky land values hadn't skyrocketed, or the Circle W would already be subdivided and Clint would be out on his ass.

Or, put another way, if George got upset with Clint for some reason, any reason at all, he could be canned. Then no telling what would happen to Tuck, and José, the cook, and Jed and Denny, the ranch hands who helped take care of the place. George might sell all the horses and let the ranch go to seed. So Clint had to pretend that this TV thing was a good idea. For the first time, George had seemed pleased that the land had an actual ranch sitting on it.

"Hey, Tuck, I have some business to discuss with you." Clint leaned against the top rail of the round pen and watched Tuck work Gabriel at the end of a lunge line.

"What's that?" Tuck made a little chirping noise to keep the horse cantering in a circle. Then he took a look at Clint. "You sure are gussied up. You planning on getting hitched today?"

"No. The outfit's part of my new plan. When this TV lady arrives, I'm going to tell her I'm not a cowboy, never have been a cowboy. I'm going to say I handle the business end of the ranch but you're in charge of the physical running of the operation."

"Good luck on putting over that whopper." Tuck

slowed Gabriel to a trot. "Even in those clothes, you look like a cowboy to me."

"That's because you know me. She doesn't. She doesn't know much of anything about anything, and I want to keep it that way. So how about it? Will you go along with whatever I tell her? And will you clue in the other guys?"

Tuck nodded as he watched Gabriel circling the pen. "It won't work, but I'll go along, and I'll spread the word. So you're definitely not entering her contest?"

Clint snorted, which startled Gabriel into breaking stride. "Nope."

"Some people around here are real excited about this contest." Tuck turned slowly with the motion of the horse. "They see it as the road to riches."

"They couldn't pay me enough to prance around on TV. I mean, would you do it?"

"Depends on the stakes, I guess. Anyhow, some vehicle's kicking up a cloud of dust on the road, so I imagine that's your TV people."

Clint glanced over his shoulder. Oh, joy. He sighed and tried to cheer himself up with the thought that the whole episode would be over by the day after tomorrow. Then life at the Circle W could return to normal.

He walked toward the front of the ranch house, determined to be as gracious as possible without letting this TV woman take over. He got there as a white van pulled around the circular drive and parked in front of the house.

The woman who hopped down from the passenger side was shorter and skinnier than he'd imagined from watching her on TV. Mostly skinnier, anyway. Her breasts were quite impressive, not that it mattered to him one way or the other. Her outfit, though, was exactly what he might have expected.

She wore a rhinestone-studded denim shirt over a scoop-neck top that showed plenty of cleavage, a pair of tight cropped jeans also studded with rhinestones, and backless red shoes with pointed toes. The tooling on the red leather was probably supposed to make them look sort of like boots.

"Hi, there." She walked toward him, her hand outstretched. "I'm Meg Delancy, from 'Meg and Mel in the Morning'."

He'd intended to be suave. He'd intended to be slightly nonchalant, as if he met TV celebrities every day and he couldn't get very excited about this one. But her smile blinded him. He hadn't been prepared for that smile to go right through him and make him weak in the knees.

Despite her ridiculous outfit, despite her plan to turn the noble Circle W into a media circus, despite his resentment of her intrusion into his peaceful way of life, he was dazzled. "I'm…uh…Clint…uh…Walker."

"Now there's a name right out of television Westerns. Wasn't Clint Walker the star of *Cheyenne?*"

"My dad loved the show." He shook her incredibly soft hand and cursed himself for acting like a teenager with a crush.

"Glad to meet you, Mr. Walker. I must say I expected jeans and a Stetson. You'd be right at home on Madison Avenue."

"Well, I don't…my foreman, Tucker Benson, he's the cowboy around here. I'm a business-school major." That last part was true. Unfortunately his shiny new degree had been no good when it had come to pulling the ranch out of the red.

"Not everyone's cut out to be a cowboy, Mr. Walker."

"You can call me Clint." The words were out before he knew it. Sheesh. And he'd promised himself not to be overly friendly, just polite. *Mr. Walker* would have suited that plan perfectly.

"I'll do that." She hit him with The Smile again before gesturing to the small, wiry guy who climbed from the driver's side of the van. "This is my cameraman, Jamie Cranston. Jamie, this is Clint Walker, our host."

"Good to meet you." Jamie's handshake was firm. Then he glanced up at the sky. "We still have some daylight left, so if you don't mind, I'd like to get footage of the ranch. Do you have a bunkhouse?"

"Yes. Behind the main house, over by the corrals." Clint thought about the usual condition of the bunkhouse. "But the place isn't very—"

"I'm not interested in a Hollywood bunkhouse," Jamie said. "I want a real one. If you have a spare bed down there, I'd like to hang out with your ranch hands."

Clint hadn't figured on this at all. He'd made up both spare rooms in the main house, planning that she'd take one and her cameraman the other. If the cameraman slept in the bunkhouse, then he and Meg Delancy would be in the big house...alone.

"It's the best way to get local color," Jamie said.

Clint could hardly object on the grounds that he wanted Jamie around to chaperone. "Sure, I guess that would be okay." Jed and Denny would be only too happy to have the cameraman there. They both planned on entering the competition, so hanging out with Jamie would seem like a good way to gain an advantage.

"Great," Jamie said. "Meg, if you want to grab your suitcase and laptop, I'll just drive the live truck around to the bunkhouse and unload my camera."

"What live truck?" Clint glanced around, expecting God-knows-what to materialize.

"That's what we call the van with all the communications gear in it," Meg said.

"Oh. Right." Clint acted as if he'd known that all along.

"We don't have a whole lot of time here," Jamie said, "so I want to make use of every minute."

"Sounds like a plan." Meg headed to the back of the van, where Jamie had already opened the doors.

Clint glanced inside and saw enough electronic equipment to choke a stable of horses. He supposed they'd need all that to beam stuff to New York, or whatever the plan was.

Meg pulled out a rolling suitcase the size of a hay bale and plunked it to the ground. Then she hooked the strap of a computer case over her shoulder. "I'm all set, Jamie. Take off."

"Thanks, Meg. See you two later."

Full-blown panic set in. Clint hadn't pictured being stuck alone with Meg, especially not five minutes after she'd arrived. "Dinner's at the main house at six," he called after Jamie. But that left two incredibly long hours. What in hell's name could he do with this big-city woman for two hours?

"I'll be back at six." With that, Jamie hopped in the van and drove around behind the house.

Clint watched the van until it was out of sight.

"Well, Clint. Here we are."

Her voice tickled his eardrums in a most unsettling way. A sexual way. This was not good, not good at all. He was supposed to think of her as the enemy. Instead he was more fascinated by the minute.

He glanced down at her. "I guess we should…go on in."

"I really appreciate you putting me up. I'm sure it's an imposition."

"No, not at all." He reached for her suitcase and lifted it so it would clear the steps. The thing felt as if she'd packed it full of anvils, but he would have expected her to come loaded to the gills with fancy clothes. In fact, she was exactly as he'd pictured her. And instead of being repulsed, he was wildly attracted. It defied logic, but there was the truth of it.

"I'll show you to your room." As he trudged up the steps with her bulging suitcase, he pictured her sleeping in that room, then pictured how close her room was to his. Damned if that didn't get him extremely excited.

2

THE LANDSCAPE DIDN'T provide much inspiration for Meg as she followed Clint into the house, but the view in the foreground was outstanding. She could look at buns like that all day. And those eyes of his—were they really that blue, or was it his tan that made them seem that way?

The tan had her speculating about his claim that he was only a business major and didn't mess with ranch work. Unless he had tennis courts hidden away somewhere, she'd bet money he did some manual labor around this place. And he moved like a guy who was used to physical activity.

She'd known her share of desk jockeys, and Clint didn't strike her as the desk-jockey type. He struck her as the yummy type, though. Interesting that he'd deny knowing anything about the very occupation she'd come out here to showcase. Very interesting.

"Here's your room." He carried her suitcase into an antiquey sort of place, with a brass bedstead, an old pine dresser and a braided rug on the wooden floor. Shoot, there was even a rocker in the corner. Homespun City.

She spied a door on the far wall. Laying her laptop on the bed, she gestured toward the door. "I imagine that's the bathroom."

"No, that's the closet. The bathroom's across the hall."

"Oh." She hadn't walked across the hall to a bathroom since she'd lived at home with her family in Brooklyn. "Good thing I brought a bathrobe, huh?"

"Listen, if you'd be more comfortable, I could move you into my room."

The opening was too obvious to resist. "With you still in it?"

To her surprise, he turned red and cleared his throat. "I meant I'd give you my room and I'd take this one. Mine has an attached bathroom."

How adorable. He was blushing. This gig might turn out to be more fun than she'd thought back when she and Jamie had first headed down the dusty road to Nowheresville. At least the natives were extremely cute and unspoiled.

Now that she thought about it, the ultra-sophisticated types she'd met in New York didn't appeal to her all that much. This guy definitely did. Nothing could come of a fling with him, if she dared chance one, but he was the first man to flip her switches in some time. Then again, she'd been too busy for switch-flipping. And she was too busy now. But this attraction reminded her that she missed sex…a lot.

"I wouldn't dream of putting you out of your room," she said. "This room will be just fine." Or sort of fine. She noticed there was no phone in it, and more important, no television.

"I'd be happy to give you my room. I should have thought of that. Let me take five minutes to change the sheets and move out some of my stuff."

He really was sweet, and she didn't want to be a problem child, but this back and forth across the hall business didn't excite her. "Does your room have a TV?"

"No. The only TV is in the living room, and I need to warn you, the reception isn't very reliable in Sonoita. Depends on how the wind's blowing."

She stared at him, unable to imagine unreliable TV reception. She'd begun to accept the lack of shopping options, but she needed TV reception, or life as she knew it would cease to exist.

Then she had a brainstorm. "So I bet you have a DVD player, for when the reception is bad."

"Uh, no. I have an old VCR, but it's cranky. I don't use it much."

"So how do you amuse yourself at night?"

"I go to bed."

She tried not to laugh. She really tried hard, but the laugh popped out of her, anyway. God, he was adorable.

Apparently he figured out how his answer must have hit her, because he got even redder. "I didn't mean that the way it sounded."

"That's too bad. The conversation was getting really interesting." She took pity on his discomfort and decided to ease up on him. After all, she made her living trading loaded remarks, but he didn't.

The morning talk show was supposed to be spicy. That's how viewers liked it. Throwing out saucy comments had become a habit, but here was a country guy, business degree notwithstanding, who wasn't used to banter. She didn't want to scare him off, because he just might be the temporary answer to her sexual frustration.

"I shouldn't tease you," she said. "As I said before, I appreciate your willingness to put up with me for a few days. This room will be fine. Thank you for allowing me to stay in it."

"You're welcome." He edged toward the door. "Go

ahead and get settled in. I'll…go take care of some things."

"I hate to be a royal pain, but I would love some coffee. I have a caffeine habit that won't quit, and my gauge is on the low side."

He looked relieved to have something he could provide. "I'll make some coffee, then."

"Great. You, uh, wouldn't have a way to make espresso, by any chance?"

"No. Just plain coffee."

"That's fine. Great. Plain coffee is great."

"Want me to bring it to you?"

"No, no. I'll come and get it." God, he must really think she was a princess. Maybe she was and hadn't realized it. She'd never been in this kind of environment before, so she wasn't sure how Annie Oakley would have handled things.

"I have a better idea. I'll take it out to the porch."

"Sounds good." She vaguely remembered walking across a porch but she'd been concentrating on his tush at the time. As for sitting on a porch, she was a virgin. It sounded as boring as staring at a blank TV screen, but she had to take his presence into consideration. That, of course, was assuming he'd join her in this porch-sitting experience.

"Then I'll see you in a few minutes." He started down the hall and paused to glance back at her. "Do you take cream?"

"Nonfat milk." Somehow she just knew he wouldn't have it.

"Uh, all I have is half-and-half."

"Then I can drink it black." She'd already blown her eating program with a fast-food hamburger for lunch. Most people didn't appreciate how a TV personality had to monitor weight gain. Mona had a height advantage and was thin as a strip of linguini, besides. Being a short person, Meg showed any weight gain immediately. She couldn't afford to look tubby compared to Mona.

"Then black it is." Clint disappeared down the hall.

Once he was gone, Meg unzipped her suitcase and thought about her host as she started hanging up her clothes. This might be her chance to have a fling away from the hotbed of gossip that was New York City. When she'd dreamed of a career in television, she'd envisioned dating as part of it. She hadn't realized how her visibility might hamper her social life, and sexual frustration was becoming a constant companion.

This guy might be the perfect solution, if he had any interest in her at all. But she'd have to find out more about him and assure herself that he could be discreet. Then again, he might have a girlfriend. A man who looked like Clint would likely have a girlfriend. Damn.

Sighing, she contemplated her wrinkled clothes. What she wouldn't give for valet service. Or even a cleaners within five miles who could do a fast press job on these duds. But she knew enough not to ask about cleaners. If TV reception was dicey, a one-hour cleaning service would be out of the question. She hoped Clint owned an iron and ironing board.

It sure was quiet around here. She hadn't noticed the silence so much while she'd been with Clint, because he'd claimed a fair amount of her attention. Now that he was out of the room, the stillness was spooky. Some little bird was tweeting outside the window, and she could faintly hear the sound of Clint making coffee in the kitchen, but other than that, nothing. No cars, no sirens, no machinery clanking away.

She looked around to see if the room had so much as a radio. No radio. But when she opened a dresser drawer to put her underwear away, the scent of cedar drifted up. Now that was nice. Cedar-lined drawers. She'd thought about doing that once in her apartment, but she wasn't the Susie Homemaker type, so the thought had died quickly.

After hanging up as many clothes as she expected to need for this leg of the trip, she pulled out her cosmetics bag and walked over to explore the bathroom. The place was basic, but adequate. And sparkling clean. She wondered if Clint had a cleaning lady or if he was responsible for the condition of everything. In any event, someone had made an effort on her behalf, and she appreciated that.

She'd brought along a lighted makeup mirror, in case she'd need it. Pulling the chain that turned on the light beside the sink, she concluded that she'd need it. And as usual in old bathrooms, there was precious little counter space, although the counter was kind of pretty—tile in a bright flowered pattern that looked as though it had come from Mexico. She could handle this situation, so long as the hot water worked.

Automatic reflex made her glance in the mirror. Not surprisingly, her nose was shiny and her lipstick nearly gone. She reached for her cosmetics bag, another automatic reaction. Meg Delancy, television personality, always had to look good. But as she zipped open the bag, the aroma of coffee drifted down the hall.

To heck with repairing her makeup. She needed coffee, and Clint probably didn't mind if her makeup was perfect or not. Men hardly ever noticed those things unless the problem was dramatic, like raccoon eyes. She also suspected that perfect makeup might be another signal that she was, in fact, a princess. She'd rather he didn't think of her that way.

Realistically, she shouldn't care how he perceived her. But she'd always cared about stuff like that, even when the person in question wasn't a six-foot hunk of delicious manhood. Given that Clint fit that description, she had even more reason to want his good opinion. From the looks of things, Clint might be the only entertainment the place had to offer.

Back in the living room she took a minute to glance around. The TV was only a nineteen-inch. She'd bet that both the TV and the VCR had been sitting in that same spot when Clinton was elected.

Besides that, the TV was in a far corner of the room and none of the furniture faced in that direction. Instead, the worn leather sofa and chairs had a great view of an enormous stone fireplace. You could put a pretzel-vendor's cart inside it.

The scent of wood smoke lingered in the air, and ashes under the grate told her Clint had used the fireplace recently, maybe last night. Horse-related books and magazines lay on the well-used pine coffee table.

Meg felt as if she'd landed on Mars. If Clint indeed had a girlfriend, then she'd be left with the games on her laptop. She couldn't imagine an evening spent looking at a fire and/or reading about horses, probably with no sound except the popping of the wood. She'd go nuts.

Or maybe she was just cranky from lack of caffeine. The remedy for that was waiting for her out on the porch, so she opened the front door and stepped outside.

Clint had been sitting on one of the rustic wooden chairs but he got up when she appeared, his coffee mug in one hand. "Everything all right?"

"Fine." The air was cooler than it had been before, but a hot cup of coffee should keep her from getting chilled. "The coffee smells great." She walked over to the chair that was obviously meant for her, sat down and reached for the mug he'd set on a table between them.

Warm, fragrant vapor rose up as she lifted it to her lips. She took a sip. It was without doubt the strongest coffee she'd ever tasted in her life, and she'd had some mean espressos over the years. She tried not to choke.

"I make it strong," he said.

"Yes, you do." She swallowed and wondered if it would devour her stomach lining in five seconds flat. One thing was for sure, it would satisfy her caffeine craving.

"Sure you don't want some of that half-and-half?"

"Oh, heck, why not? You only live once, right?" If she drank the whole mug of coffee without something to cut the motor-oil consistency, her days could be numbered.

"Be right back." Clint left his mug on the small wooden table between their chairs and went inside.

After he left she peered into his cup to see if he'd diluted the coffee with half-and-half. He hadn't. He must have a cast-iron stomach.

It was also a nice flat stomach. As a veteran guy-watcher, Meg paid attention to those things. From what she could see, everything about Clint Walker was premium-grade.

He returned with the carton of half-and-half and handed it to her. "I apologize if the coffee's too strong. When you asked about espresso I figured I was safe to make it my normal way."

"It's a good, hefty brew, that's for sure." She poured a serious dollop of half-and-half into her mug, nearly causing it to overflow. "How many cups do you drink in a day?"

"Oh, I don't know. Maybe eight or ten." He settled back in his chair.

"Eight or ten? I'm amazed you're not jitterbugging across the porch!" Maybe he was so hopped up on caffeine that he didn't notice how boring his life was. Yet he seemed steady as a rock, no tremors.

He shrugged. "I'm one of those people who's not real susceptible to caffeine. And when you've grown up drinking chuckwagon...see, my dad drank strong coffee, too."

"Your dad was a rancher?"

"The best."

"But you didn't follow in his footsteps?" She'd slipped into interview mode, another habit she couldn't seem to break.

He looked away. "Pretty hard to do. Those days are disappearing."

She knew an evasive answer when she heard one. On the show, people reacted that way when they were hiding something. "Then I guess it's a good thing I made it out here before the cowboys are all gone."

"Right."

Interesting how much emotion could be packed into one word. She was used to reading inflections, gauging reactions. He didn't like this contest, but why not? If he was the business major he claimed to be, then he should appreciate good old-fashioned marketing techniques.

She decided to hit the problem head-on. "You wish we weren't doing this."

His blue eyes became unreadable. "I'm happy to help out."

"Bullshit! You don't like this cowboy contest one bit, although I'm not sure why. You're not a cowboy."

His mouth twitched, as if he might be holding back a grin. "Right."

"What's so funny?"

"I'll bet you don't get to say *bullshit* on the air." The grin began to peek through.

"No, I don't, but you're evading the issue." And damned if that didn't fascinate the hell out of her.

"Yeah, I am."

"Why?"

His gaze was assessing. Finally he seemed to come to a decision about her. "George Forester owns the Circle W now. What he wants, he gets."

Her heart softened. "He bought your family home out from under you, didn't he?"

"That's business. My dad couldn't afford the place anymore."

"And your dad…he's…"

"Died five years ago. Mom a couple of years before that."

"I'm sorry." So this complicated guy had dealt with his share of sorrow. She was a sucker for a man who'd weathered pain.

"In some ways, it might be better. Their way of life was getting harder to maintain. Dad died shortly after he sold to George. I think losing Mom and then the ranch took the heart out of him."

Meg cradled her coffee cup, getting all the warmth from it that she could. The lower the sun sank, the colder it became. But the coffee had surely taken care of her caffeine deficit. She was ready to tackle anything or anyone. Like this hottie, for instance. "I can imagine how hard it must be to work for something all your life and then lose it."

"Yep." He took a swallow of his coffee. "I'm sure you've paid your dues to get where you are."

"Uh-huh."

"Looks like you're in good shape, though."

She had a choice of turning his comment into something suggestive or taking it the way it was meant. Until she knew whether he had a girlfriend or not, she was safer with option two. "Not as good as it might seem. The woman who's filling in for me on the show would love to steal my spot."

"Do you think she can?"

"It depends on how she does while I'm gone." She was grateful to him for taking her seriously instead of thinking she was paranoid. Maybe a guy who'd lost his family ranch understood that sometimes the worst really did happen. "The thing is…" She paused and considered how candid she wanted to be about the falling ratings and the rumors about lack of chemistry between her and Mel.

When she didn't continue, Clint said nothing—didn't ask her what she'd been about to say or prompt her to keep on talking. Instead he sipped his coffee and looked out across the valley.

That was the unique thing about those blue eyes of his, she realized now. They were the eyes of a man used to distance and open spaces. He seemed very comfortable with all that emptiness stretching out in front of him. He was comfortable with silence.

She tried seeing the landscape through his eyes, a view he'd known since he was born. There was a kind of peacefulness to looking out over miles and miles of uninhabited land. She wasn't used to peacefulness, but a person would be used to it if he grew up that way.

And she could understand wanting to hang onto a place you were used to. Her parents didn't want to leave their bungalow in Brooklyn, even though she now had extra money and could help them buy a nicer house. So the extra money she was earning had started piling up. That might be a good thing, because she could soon be unemployed.

"Those big mountains across the valley are the Santa Ritas," Clint said.

She hadn't asked, but it might be good to know for the broadcast. "How about the mountains in back of the ranch?"

"The Mustangs."

"Perfect." She was already composing her intro in her head. *I'm talking to you from the historic Circle W Ranch, which is tucked right up against the Mustang Mountains.*

She'd better check out the historic part, though. "How old is this place?"

"The ranch itself, or this house?"

"The ranch."

"My great-grandfather, Clemson Walker, bought the land in nineteen-twenty."

Definitely historic. "I can see why it's rough to have it pass out of the family, then."

"I'm adjusting."

But not well, she'd bet. "Forgive me if this is too nosey, but wouldn't it be less painful to get the heck out of here? I would think living on the ranch and knowing it belonged to some rich dude from New York would be a constant heartache."

At first it seemed as if he wouldn't answer. Then he sighed. "I've told myself that, but if I left, George might let the place fall apart. He's only interested in subdividing when the land value's high enough for him."

"But if he's going to subdivide eventually, then so what? Aren't you only delaying the inevitable by staying on?" She'd always been the type who wanted a bandage yanked off fast and bad news delivered immediately. Her motto was to get the agony over with ASAP.

"You're right, of course. Stupid as it sounds, I keep hoping for a miracle so I can buy it back before that happens."

"Into lottery tickets, are you?"

"Yeah, I do that."

She thought of George Forester, a paunchy guy she'd met once at a cocktail party. For him this ranch was mere financial speculation, a chance to increase his considerable fortune if he timed the sale correctly. But for Clint, this was about hanging onto his heritage. She wanted Clint to win the lottery.

"You getting cold?" he asked.

"Why?"

"You shivered."

"I guess I am a bit chilly." But sitting here talking with Clint, she'd ignored the cold so that they could stay on the porch a little longer. Purple and blue shadows crept over the valley, and even though she wouldn't want to spend a whole lot of time looking at them, they were kind of pretty.

"Let's go in. José will be starting supper any minute, and I need to get the fire ready."

"José cooks on a wood stove?" If so, she should get Jamie up here on the double, to take footage of that happening.

Clint laughed. "Nope. My grandmother used to, but we've had electricity for a long time. Dinner and the fire aren't connected, except that I like to have a fire in the evenings, and if I set it up now, all I have to do is light it later."

"Oh." She had the insane desire to hang around and watch him build the fire, maybe because the cowboys in her dad's beloved Westerns were forever building fires. It seemed like such a manly chore. "Then maybe I'll go in my room and start working on my script for tomorrow."

"What time will you do the first broadcast?"

"Early. We have time on the bird at seven-thirty."

He laughed. "That's not early, but what in God's name is *time on the bird?*"

She pointed skyward. "Satellite. We only get so long to beam up there from the live truck, or as Jamie loves to call it, the nest. We can't miss that time, or we're screwed. But we'll try not to disturb you."

"You won't. I'm up by five."

"Why? I thought your foreman ran things around here."

He looked like a little boy with his hand in the cookie jar. "Uh, I'm just an early riser."

Yes, he was definitely playing games with her and hiding significant information. Okay, girlfriend or no girlfriend, he deserved to get zinged for that. "I like that in a man," she said. "Someone who'd be up and ready for anything." Then she waited for him to blush, the way he had earlier.

Instead his eyes darkened, his nostrils flared, and his voice dropped to a sexy drawl. "You might want to be more careful how you use that tongue of yours. It could get you into trouble."

Her pulse hammered. He was flirting with her! That might mean he didn't have a girlfriend. That would be a very exciting discovery. She decided to push the envelope a little more. "Maybe I like a little trouble now and then."

His smile was slow and full of meaning. "Lady, nothing around here qualifies as *little.*"

She gulped. Maybe she'd underestimated this guy. But

she was determined to have the last word. "I'm delighted to hear it. I'm a girl who likes her thrills super-sized. Now, if you'll excuse me, I need to do some work before dinner." Then she whisked through the front door and hurried down the hall.

Back in her room, she closed the door and stood there breathing hard. Good grief. She'd imagined herself in control of the situation, and then wham! Tables turned. She'd better decide for sure how she wanted this to go between them before he stole the decision right from under her...on top of her...and behind her. Damn.

3

Clint didn't follow Meg into the house right away. He didn't trust himself not to go down that hall after her. He shouldn't have said what he had, but she brought out that side of him and made him think along dangerous lines. What a spitfire. An exciting, arousing bundle of woman. He wondered if she'd meant any of it, or if toying with guys was what she did for amusement.

Probably the latter. He'd be well advised to keep away from someone who had Manhattan by the tail. Hell, he'd seen her picture on the front of one of those celebrity magazines at the barber shop the other day. The last thing he wanted was to get mixed up with someone who had that kind of visibility.

He shouldn't be fooled because she'd sat on the porch with him and shared some conversation over a cup of coffee. She didn't have anything else to do at the moment. Still, she got his blood pumping more than any woman had in a long while.

She was also starting to see right through him. He didn't know if she'd figure everything out before she left, but she already had a pretty good idea that a business degree wasn't the whole story with him. He hadn't counted on her being this sharp.

Apparently he'd made the mistake of watching her for

five minutes on TV and thinking he had her pegged. She was more complicated than that, more fascinating in person than she had been as an image on a television screen. But no matter how attracted he was, he'd be better off leaving well enough alone.

He had enough troubles without making matters worse. No telling how George would react if he found out Clint had been fooling around with the TV lady. And that was assuming she'd allow any fooling around. She might have no intention of following through on any of her suggestive comments.

But he wasn't sure about that, and it drove him crazy, wondering. Ah, to hell with it. This would all be over in two days, and he'd be back to helping Tuck with Gabriel, renting horses to greenhorns and buying lottery tickets every week. With that thought firmly in mind, he went around to the side of the house, gathered an armload of firewood, and took it in through the kitchen door.

José, a guy who clearly liked his own cooking way too much, was already slicing and dicing for what looked like his famous enchiladas. Hired when Clint's mother couldn't handle the job anymore, José had been in charge of the Circle W kitchen for enough years that he felt the kitchen was his to command.

He glanced up from the cutting board. "Where's the TV lady?"

"In her room working on her script for tomorrow."

José's dark eyes shone with excitement. "Do I get to meet her?"

"Sure, you can meet her. I thought you'd be having dinner with us, like you always do."

"Oh, no, I wouldn't want to do that. I know myself. I'd dump my food in my lap while I was busy staring at her."

"Aw, no, you wouldn't. She's not that scary."

"Boss, she was in *People* magazine. I've never come face-to-face with anyone who was in *People*. I wouldn't know how to act. I'd embarrass myself, for sure. I'd—"

"You'd better stop chopping that tomato. It's mushed into a pulp already."

José glanced at the chopping board. "See? Just thinking about her I murdered this poor tomato. No, just introduce me before you start eating, and I'll go back in the kitchen and quiver for ten minutes."

Clint laughed. "Okay. Your decision. But I really don't think—"

The kitchen door opened and Tuck poked in his head. "Jed and Denny have voted to eat down at the bunkhouse tonight instead of up here. So give us a call when the food's ready and I'll come get it."

José nodded. "I'll bet I know why. They're all nervous about the TV lady and don't think their manners are good enough."

"I guess so." Tuck shook his head. "Me, I couldn't care less one way or the other, but they made me promise to stay down there with them and act like we do this all the time. They're scared, but they don't want her to know it."

Clint was having trouble comprehending it. Jed, an accomplished steer wrestler, was a bull of a guy who'd never seemed afraid of anything. Redheaded Denny always had girls hanging around and he'd been the first to sign up for the contest. "Are you saying that José, Jed and Denny are all too nervous to be in the same room with her?"

"Seems like," Tuck said. "Now, the cameraman, he's a different story. They're real tight with him already. He's eating with them tonight, too, by the way."

"So it's only Meg and me having our meal here in the house?" Clint pictured the two of them at a table big enough for eight. He'd imagined all the hands there, as they usually were, along with Tuck, and the cameraman. Just two of them at that big table would look silly.

José gave him a pleading glance. "You can handle it, boss. You've been to college and everything. The rest of us are country boys."

"But Jed and Denny are entering the contest! Don't they want to get to know her better? They'd have a head start over the guys who won't show up until tomorrow morning."

"I tried to tell them that, too," Tuck said. "They're sure they'll just ruin their chances. They'd rather wait until tomorrow, when they'll be showing off their cowboying skills. They're afraid to have a meal with her, where table manners and such would come into play."

Clint groaned. "This is getting more ridiculous by the minute."

"I know," Tuck said. "But that's the situation."

Clint had a mental picture of him sitting at one end of the long dining table and Meg at the other. Even sitting across from each other width-wise would leave an awful lot of empty space. She'd want to know if he usually ate by himself at that table and he couldn't explain without saying that his hands were too chicken to join her for dinner.

"Tell you what, José," he said. "Meg and I will set up in front of the fireplace instead of the dining room."

"Okay, boss. You want me to bring out the card table? It's a little rickety, though."

"No." Clint was making this up as he went along. A rickety card table was not what he wanted, either. Somewhere in the past couple of hours he'd started worrying about Meg Delancy's opinion. That wasn't a good thing, but it was true.

"We'll use the coffee table," Clint said. "That round slab of oak will hold anything." He'd stood on it a few times when he needed to reach something taller than he was.

"And you'll make a royal mess," José said. "It's enchiladas tonight, don't forget, and that's a long way from the plate to your mouth. Not that you're sloppy, boss, but I can see enchilada sauce all down your shirt if you're sitting on the couch and eating off the coffee table."

"Then sit on the floor," Tuck said. "Take a couple of cushions off the couch and sit on the floor. Like they do at those ethnic restaurants."

José grinned. "Good idea! Yeah, that'll be real cozy."

"I'll help you set it up." Tuck headed for the living room.

Clint had obviously lost control of the situation and didn't know how to get it back. But *cozy* was way more intimate than he'd had in mind. Eating at the big table would have looked ridiculous, which was why he'd thought of eating in front of the fire. He hadn't worked out the details, though, and all of a sudden he was stuck with *cozy*.

Although he could countermand Tuck's idea, he wouldn't. The guy had become a substitute father, and Clint had never felt like Tuck's boss. He respected his foreman more than anyone he knew.

So, instead of objecting, he followed Tuck into the living room to supervise and make sure it wouldn't be too damned cozy. He was already worried enough about how this shared lodging would work out and what the possible repercussions would be.

By the time Clint arrived in the living room and

dumped his load of firewood on the hearth, Tuck had already moved the couch back from the coffee table. The little guy had amazing strength for his size.

"Okay, we'll take this cushion, here, and put it right here." Tuck pulled a square seat cushion from the couch and plopped it on the braided rug right behind the coffee table.

"Now it looks like we're camping," Clint said. "Maybe I should just invite her to the Steak Out and be done with it."

"You can't do that." Tuck pulled another cushion from the couch and positioned it on the floor right next to the first cushion.

"Why not?" Clint leaned down and moved the second cushion so it was a good three feet from the first one.

"Because you would break José's heart, that's why. He's been planning his specialty enchilada dinner ever since he found out the TV lady was coming. You know he's mighty proud of his enchiladas." Tuck moved the first cushion again so it was touching the second.

"I hadn't realized he planned the menu just for her." Clint moved his cushion around the table so it was another three feet away.

"Well, he did." Tuck surveyed the arrangement and moved the first cushion up next to the second one again.

Clint moved his cushion again too. "Then it looks like we'll eat here in front of the fire."

"Looks like, although I can't figure out what you're doing with these two cushions." Tuck moved his so it followed the other around the table. "We started out with them facing the fire, and now you'll be sitting with your backs to it. I don't get the point of that."

Clint reached for both cushions, hauled them up and brought them back around behind the coffee table. "One of us is sitting here." He dropped the cushion. "And the other one w-a-a-a-y over here." He walked around the table and dropped the other cushion.

"Why? Does she smell bad?"

"I hope not." Meg walked into the room. "I took a shower this morning, and my deodorant should still be working."

Tuck turned scarlet. Clint had never seen his foreman blush before, and he was so fascinated that he forgot his manners.

Meg walked forward, hand outstretched, smile at the ready. "I'm Meg Delancy. Feel free to tell me if I need to hit the showers. I don't get insulted easily."

Tuck's throat worked, but he was speechless.

Clint understood the reaction. Up close, she was damned impressive. A jolt of sexual awareness hit him every time she came near.

"You smell fine," he said. Wonderful, in fact, he realized. He hadn't thought about it earlier because he'd been too absorbed in how she looked, which was also wonderful. "Meg, this is Tucker Benson, my foreman."

Tuck cleared his throat and shook her hand. "Meased to pleet you. Uh, what I mean is—"

"I'm pleased to meet you, too, Tucker." She sailed right past his awkwardness. "Clint says you run the operation here at the Circle W. He made it very clear that he doesn't know one end of a horse from the other."

"Uh, yeah, well…I do my best." Tuck glanced over at Clint.

Clint returned the look, silently warning Tuck not to get him into any trouble.

"And I'm sorry about the smart remark," Tuck continued. "I was teasing Clint about the cushions."

"Cushions?" Meg glanced over at the couch and then down at the floor. "Are you two looking for loose change or something?"

Clint sighed. He never should have suggested eating in front of the fire, because he didn't have the right setup for it. If he could think of a logical explanation for the cushions on the floor, they could go back to the concept of eating at the huge dining table. It was the lesser of two stupidities.

"Clint thought it'd be nice for the two of you to eat in front of the fire," Tuck said.

"Or maybe not," Clint said. "Maybe the dining room is the best choice. Wherever you'd be the most comfortable."

Meg looked confused. "I heard you tell Jamie dinner was at six. So I thought he'd—"

"Jamie's having a great time down at the bunkhouse," Clint said. "So he's joining the rest of the boys down there tonight."

"Oh." Meg's hesitation was so slight as to be almost unnoticeable. "Was there…anyone else you wanted to invite to dinner?"

Clint didn't know if she'd asked because the setting was too dorky or because she was worried about spending more time alone with him. "Like who?"

"Um, maybe your girlfriend?"

Oh, God, did she *want* him to have a girlfriend? If so, she was out of luck. "No current girlfriend," he said.

"Well, then, let's eat in front of the fire. Sounds fabulous."

Maybe he was projecting, but he thought she sounded nervous or something about the idea. After all, she'd been taunting him and now she might be worried that he'd expect her to follow through. He expected zip from her, but he couldn't very well say that now.

Between José's hopes for his enchiladas and the bunk-house gang wimping out, it looked as if Clint would be eating in front of the fire tonight, alone with Meg. He would have to look and not touch. And he wanted to touch…everything. But he would behave himself, even if it killed him.

"IS THERE ANYTHING I can do to help?" Meg doubted it, but the manners her mother had drilled into her prompted her to ask. Meanwhile she was digesting the news that Clint had no girlfriend. Clear sailing. Her heart raced as she contemplated the possibilities.

"I think everything's under control," Clint said, though he didn't look as if he really thought so. "I'll clean out the old ashes before I build the fire."

"Then I'll, um, watch." Meg felt a little shaky, so she settled down on the one remaining couch cushion.

"And I'll get on out to the bunkhouse," Tuck said. "I think the poker game's about to start."

"Just don't keep Jamie up too late." Meg had to remind herself of her purpose in being here. "We have to be on the bird at 7:30."

"The *what?*" Tuck frowned in obvious confusion.

Clint interrupted his shoveling of the ashes. "The bird's the TV satellite," he said. "They rent time on it so they can do a remote broadcast from the live truck, which is that white van they came in."

Meg suppressed a smile. Clint seemed quite proud of his newfound info. And he was about twenty times more appealing now that she knew he wasn't involved with someone.

"Interesting." Tucker acted as if he wanted to hang around a little longer. "So tomorrow, when you broadcast from here, are you planning to have anybody besides you on camera?"

Forcing herself to concentrate on her job instead of Clint, Meg made a spur-of-the-minute decision. "I would love to interview you for a couple of minutes, Tucker. Would you be willing to do that?" She'd originally planned to interview Clint, but he didn't seem to own the right outfit for the broadcast. Tucker was too old to qualify for the contest, but he'd add some great color to the first segment.

The foreman looked quite pleased with the prospect. "You can call me Tuck, and I expect I could work that in. Just tell me what to do."

"I'll ask you a few questions about ranching, how you got into this line of work. I'm trusting Jamie to set up the shot and the lighting, so tell him I want to interview you and he'll decide the best location. If you could be ready about seven, we can do a little practice run."

"All right." Tuck's smile gleamed white against his tanned skin. "Sounds good. I'll see you in the morning, then."

After he left, Meg glanced toward the fireplace where Clint was shoveling the last of the ashes into a bucket near the fire. He looked terrific doing it, too. And he had no girlfriend. "I hope you don't mind if I interview your foreman. Maybe I should have asked you before I suggested it to him."

"That's fine. Tuck's the one to talk to about the ranch." He tapped the last of the ashes from the shovel and replaced it in the holder with the rest of the fireplace tools. "Like I said, I'm no expert. He is."

Something about this scenario didn't add up. "I'm curious as to how you fill your time here, if you don't spend it on ranch chores?"

He stood, but he didn't turn around. His answer was a

little slow in coming. "I keep the books. We run a boarding and training stable here. We also offer trail rides."

"I see." She couldn't imagine an accounting system that would require a full-time effort. But she could imagine this man naked, and the concept made her drool.

He turned toward her. "And I, um, do a little consulting."

"Oh, really? On what?" Maybe she could get him to consult with her on this little problem of sexual deprivation.

"Business. Business consulting, for the merchants around here."

Considering the number of merchants she'd noticed on the way here, that wouldn't occupy him for long, either. "Sounds like a nice relaxed life."

"Yep. Relaxed, that's me." He stood and hooked his thumbs through his belt loops.

That stance was all it took for her to be convinced. Instantly she pictured him in jeans and a yoked Western shirt, boots and a worn Stetson. This man was a cowboy, her fantasy man. And he didn't want her to know.

"You must even have time for hobbies," she said.

"Some."

"Such as?"

"Oh...birdwatching."

If he was a birdwatcher she was Jay Leno. But she pretended to believe him. "I've always thought that would be fun, hiking in sensible shoes with a pair of binoculars around my neck. But I don't have the time. What's the most unusual bird you've ever spotted?"

He met her gaze. "I can't believe you're interested in birdwatching."

"I can't believe you are, either." But she would be

thrilled if he could be interested in her for the next couple of days.

"Maybe I made it up because I don't want you to know I'm a lazy son-of-a-gun who whiles away the day on the front porch with a can of beer in his hand."

"Try again." She'd glimpsed great muscle definition under his white shirt. "You're too fit for me to believe you lounge around drinking beer all day. I say you're a working cowboy, and for some reason you don't want me to know that. I'm assuming it has to do with the contest. Trust me, if you don't want to be in it, I won't coerce you. And I won't sic George Forester on you, if that's what you're worried about."

He stood there looking at her, his blue eyes giving away nothing. "I'd better go get the cook, José. He wanted to meet you."

"You're going to keep me guessing, aren't you?"

"Yep." Then he walked out of the room.

She felt like throwing something. She would smoke him out, though. On the job she was known for her ability to coax people into spilling their secrets. Clint was going to tell his, even if she had to seduce them out of him. And she could consider that option without guilt now…because he had no girlfriend.

4

AS CLINT WALKED through the dining room into the kitchen in search of José, he felt no sense of victory. She was winning this game of hide-and-seek, and they both knew it. When he'd planned to fool her, he'd forgotten that she interviewed people for a living. She was trained to dig until she found the truth.

If she hadn't figured out that he was lying to her about his cowboying skills, she would know it very soon. And maybe it didn't matter. His half-ass disguise succeeded in sending the message that he didn't want to be part of her ridiculous contest without him having to say it out loud.

When he walked into the kitchen, José spun away from the oven where he'd been checking his enchiladas. "She's out there, huh?"

"Yep, she's out there." Really out there. He'd never known a woman this bold and sassy. He liked it too much. "Ready to go meet her?"

José gulped. "Now?"

"Why not?"

"Okay, but I need…a mission. I can't parade out there without a reason."

Clint heaved a sigh. "She's just a woman."

"That's like saying my triple-chocolate layer cake is just

a dessert. If she's half as gorgeous in person as she is on TV, then—"

"You've watched the show?" Although Clint had seen it once, for research purposes, he wouldn't have thought anybody else on the Circle W had bothered.

"Are you kidding? Every weekday morning! That woman is *hot*. I watch it live. The other guys watch the tape."

Clint stared at his cook and waited for him to start laughing at the little joke he was playing on his boss. "You're making this up."

"Nope. I watch it here or down in the bunkhouse, wherever I happen to be. I'm usually the one that sets up the VCR down there for the other guys, and sometimes I go down at night so I can see it again. We don't pay much attention to the program. Just her. Do you think her red hair is real or dyed?"

Clint shook his head in wonder. He had a bunkhouse full of groupies. "I have no idea."

"Jed thinks yes, but Denny, who considers himself the expert on redheads because he is one, says it's not real because she has brown eyes. Not too many true redheads have brown eyes. Me, I wouldn't care either way."

"I think the red's real." The words were out before Clint could stop them. His brain had quickly assessed her fair skin and the trace of freckles under her professionally applied makeup and had come up with the true-redhead verdict, which had then popped out of his mouth with no warning whatsoever.

"I think you're right," José said. "And no boyfriend. What a waste."

"How do you know there's no boyfriend?"

"She's always talking on the show about not having

dates. Me and the guys, we've joked about taking up a collection so one of us could fly up there and ask her out. Not that she would go. She probably doesn't have dates because she's picky."

"I can't believe she doesn't have dates." Clint pictured a new guy every week, who was then discarded like food gone stale in her refrigerator.

José shrugged. "That's what she says on the show. Mel's always teasing her about it. Maybe it's because guys are afraid to ask her out. That's what Denny thinks."

"Well, yeah. Who wants to end up in the tabloids?"

"That's what Denny says. She got famous so quick, and any guy who dates her has to know it wouldn't be a private deal for very long."

Clint gazed out the kitchen window and thought about that. For all Meg's taunting comments about liking to get into trouble, she hadn't gotten into much trouble at all since becoming a celebrity. If she had, it would be all over the rags in the grocery-store checkout line.

Maybe she'd been too focused on her career to bother with dating. He'd caught a whiff of naked ambition during their conversation on the front porch. But he wondered if she also might be a little bit lonely, a little bit frustrated. Now there was a stimulating thought.

And he needed to avoid that kind of thinking, considering they'd be alone in the house tonight.

"Uh, boss?" José waved a hand in front of Clint's eyes. "Is it still okay if I go out and meet her?"

Clint snapped out of his daze. "Of course it's okay. I specifically came back here to get you and bring you out there."

"I know, but when I asked you just now, you just stared off into space and didn't say anything, so I wondered if you'd changed your mind. Don't worry. I promise not to do anything stupid like ask her out." José looked suddenly shy. "But I sure would like her autograph."

"Then you'd better take something for her to write on."

"I have something." José held up a pot holder that looked fresh out of the box. "Bought it at the convenience store today."

"Why a pot holder?"

"Because it'll prove she ate my food. I can hang it up in the kitchen." He looked like a kid on Christmas morning as he described his plan.

Clint hated to admit he understood how José felt. Come to think of it, after watching her once on TV, he'd had to fight the urge to do it again the next morning. Just because she was here for an idiotic reason didn't cancel out her sex appeal, although he'd worked hard to stay immune. The immunity was wearing off fast, unfortunately.

"Then let's go," he said.

"Let me get the place settings. That's what I thought of while we were talking. I'll take out place mats, napkins and silverware for the coffee table. Then I have a reason for going out there."

Clint waited for José to grab a couple of straw place mats, knives, forks, spoons and two red cloth napkins. They hadn't used cloth napkins since before his mother died, but he guessed this was occasion enough.

He wondered what his folks would have thought of Meg. To his surprise, he decided they would have liked her. In spite of coming from an entirely different background, she obviously had the same strong work ethic his parents had valued. She wouldn't be where she was without that.

"All set." José tucked the place mats and napkins under

his arm, clutched the silverware in one hand and the pot holder and pen in the other. He took a deep breath, and his dark eyes sparkled. "Lead the way, boss."

Clint headed for the living room, followed by José. Their discussion in the kitchen had given him a whole new perspective on Meg's presence here. He hadn't realized he was giving his employees the thrill of a lifetime. He'd only been concerned about turning his beloved ranch into a joke. He still didn't like that part of it, but maybe some good would come out of this episode, after all.

MEG COULDN'T IMAGINE why it was taking Clint so long to bring his cook out of the kitchen to meet her. She'd picked up a copy of *Western Horseman* lying on the coffee table and was pretending to read it as she strained to hear what the two men were saying, but they kept their voices low. At one point she heard the word *hot* very distinctly, but without context she didn't know if they were talking about food or her.

She couldn't assume they were talking about her. That was a very self-centered view of life, and she'd promised herself from the beginning that if she ever made it, she wouldn't become self-centered. But realistically, what else would they be talking about, especially in such hushed tones?

And if the word *hot* had been in reference to her, then they were in there debating her babe status. At least Clint wasn't laughing hysterically at the idea that she was hot. That meant she wouldn't embarrass herself if she decided to make a move on him.

The good thing about Clint was his lack of fear. He didn't seem to be the least bit afraid of her. And he played his cards close to his vest, as her father loved to say. Now that she considered that, she might be able to assume Clint wouldn't be the type to kiss and tell.

That meant—and her heart raced at the prospect—she might actually be able to have a fling with this guy during her short stay on his ranch. He wouldn't tell and she wouldn't tell. It was only a temporary fix for her currently lousy social life, but she found herself inclined to make do with the opportunity as presented.

She glanced down at the magazine in her lap and discovered she'd flipped to an article about artificial insemination. Apparently the convenience of that method had nearly obliterated the old-fashioned way of breeding. Having the stud get up close and personal with the mare was a thing of the past. How sad.

Meg lifted her gaze as Clint ambled into the room. The poor mares had no choice in the matter, but as far as she was concerned, a good stud was worth a little temporary inconvenience.

Because Clint looked surprised to see her with the magazine, she decided to pull his chain a little bit. "Great article here on horse breeding," she said. "I've been totally engrossed."

His eyebrows lifted. Then he smiled. "Good, because there will be a quiz after dinner."

Oh, baby. That smile edged her closer to a decision. Maybe she'd be a fool not to go for it. She met his gaze head-on. "Can't wait."

The sound of someone clearing his throat reminded her that they weren't alone in the room.

Clint seemed startled, as if he'd forgotten about the heavyset Hispanic man standing behind him. "Meg, I'd like you to meet José Garcia, the cook here at the Circle W."

Meg stood and reached out her hand. "Hi, José."

José dumped everything he'd been holding on the coffee table and grabbed her hand in both of his, pumping enthusiastically. "Welcome, señorita, welcome! *Mi casa es su casa!*"

"Thank you." She'd picked up enough Spanish over the years to know that he was telling her his house was hers. She doubted that the Circle W was José's to give, but the thought was sweet.

Clint didn't seem impressed, though. He let out a snort of amusement.

José ignored him. "*Señorita*, if you would be so kind as to autograph this pot holder, I will treasure it forever." He snatched up a blue-checkered square of quilted material and a pen from the pile he'd tossed on the table.

Meg hadn't been a celebrity long enough to be weary of the autograph routine. She was thrilled that he'd asked, and signing a pot holder was definitely a first for her. "Sure, I'd love to."

José handed over the pot holder and the pen. "And if you could put down something like Thanks for the fabulous meals, Love, Meg Delancy, I'd really appreciate it."

"Why not? I'm sure they will be fabulous. Whatever's in the oven right now smells heavenly." She wrote exactly what he'd asked on the pot holder and handed it back to him. "How's that?"

"That's wonderful! *Gracias, señorita, gracias!* Now let me set up your place mats for dinner. And by the way, if you should want to work a few Spanish words into your broadcast, I'm your man."

"Thank you. I'll keep that in mind." Meg stepped aside while José bustled around the table arranging place mats and silverware. Then he folded the cloth napkins in an elaborate shape and set one in the middle of each place.

"Beautiful job on the napkins," Meg said.

"I've been practicing." José bowed in her direction.

"Your meal will be served shortly." Holding his pot holder as if it were a priceless, breakable object, he left the room.

"You don't have to work Spanish into the broadcast," Clint said the minute José was back in the kitchen. "First Tuck hints about being in it, and now José wants to help write your script. You're under no obligation to take their suggestions."

So he thought she was a pushover. Boy, did he have a lot to learn about her. She wouldn't do anything that might jeopardize her broadcast, which was all she had going for her right now in terms of keeping herself on the show.

"Don't worry," she said. "If I don't like an idea, I don't take it. There's a delicate balance in sticking to the plan and yet leaving yourself open to new possibilities."

He gazed at her. "I'll bet there is."

"Take you, for instance."

He looked startled. "What about me?"

How she loved catching him off guard. She was grateful for the year of training that had taught her how to do it so well. "You're nothing like I expected."

"What did you expect?"

"I thought you'd be a seasoned cowboy wearing worn denim, a guy who would call me ma'am every five seconds, a simple, straightforward sort of man. Instead you're all preppy and incredibly complicated. And apparently not a cowboy at all."

He studied her, his expression guarded. "Disappointed?"

"Intrigued."

"I thought you came out here looking for cowboys," he said softly.

"I did." She smiled at him. "But like I said, it's important to stay flexible."

His blue eyes darkened. "I suppose it is."

It would be such fun to tempt him and see if she could get those eyes to shine with lust. Did she dare? She lowered her voice to a husky whisper. "Are you going to build us a fire?"

He held her gaze. "Yeah. Yeah, I am."

"Care to teach me how it's done?"

He continued to look into her eyes, as if they were having a staring contest and the first one to glance away would lose. "You've never built one?" he asked in a voice roughened by what she thought must be his reaction to her.

She shook her head but continued to maintain eye contact. "But I always wanted to. Show me."

"All right. Come on over here."

A shiver of longing went through her. She'd interviewed film idols and rock stars, men with sexual charisma to burn. They'd never inspired a jolt of desire this strong.

She walked over to the hearth and crouched down beside Clint. He smelled so good, so different from the men she knew. They piled on the cologne, and their clothes picked up the scent of the city—a mixture of car exhaust, smoke and the indefinable blend of ethnic cooking odors always in the air.

By contrast, Clint gave off the fragrance of sun and wind, grass and open fields. She wanted to bury her nose against his shirt and take a big sniff.

"How about I let you do it?" he suggested. "I'll tell you how."

The rumble of his voice right beside her was a potent aphrodisiac. "Okay. What comes first?"

"Crumple up some of that newspaper and tuck it under the grate."

She did, and in the process made sure that her arm brushed his thigh. His breathing changed, and she smiled to herself. "What next?"

"Kindling—over there." He pointed to a stash of small twigs in a black bucket beside the fireplace.

She reached for the twigs.

"Wait." He caught her wrist. "I'm an idiot. You can't build this fire without gloves. You'll scratch your hands all to hell."

"I'll be fine." But she sure got a thrill out of having those strong fingers closed around her wrist. He could lead her anywhere.

"You won't be fine. You'd better let me do this." He released her and reached for a handful of twigs. "You can watch."

"That's no fun! I want to build it myself."

He sighed and glanced at her. "Then let me see if I have gloves that will fit you." He stood. "Be right back. And don't try to do anything. You'll ruin your manicure."

She blew out an impatient breath, hating to be the pampered city girl in this scene. He was right about the manicure, of course. And if she ruined it she couldn't count on Blythe, the studio makeup guru, to fix it for her before she went on the air. Her skin, hair and nails were her sole responsibility for the next two weeks, and she'd fallen out of the habit of maintaining her look by herself.

Mona, of course, would be perfect tomorrow morning, every hair in place, her manicure fresh and her makeup flawless. Meg couldn't afford to be any less gorgeous. Still, she didn't like the restrictions that imposed on her, or the way it made her seem like a high-maintenance chick.

Clint returned with a pair of cotton work gloves that looked brand new. "These will be too big." He handed them to her as he crouched down beside her again. "But it's the best I could find."

"They're great. Thanks." She put on the gloves, which gave her cartoon-character hands out of proportion with her body. The new material was stiff, making her clumsy as she reached for the twigs, but she was touched that Clint had searched for an unused pair.

After managing to grab a clump of twigs, she dropped them like pick-up sticks in the middle of the iron grate. This was fun. Camping hadn't been part of her life growing up in Brooklyn, so she'd never had a chance to sleep in a tent and cook over a fire. As much as she'd complained to Jamie about the lack of civilization around here, she'd always wondered what roughing it would be like.

"Good. Now get a bigger piece."

"How big?"

"You need a size that will rest gently on that nest of twigs without making them collapse. It should be about as big around as…oh, let's say a banana."

Or let's say the average penis. Meg studied the pile of wood on the hearth and chose a smooth stick that gave her big ideas. She couldn't help it if grasping the stick reminded her of something else, and placing it gently on the nest of twigs seemed about the most sexual image around. When a girl hadn't indulged in more than a year, she could be forgiven for thinking in those terms, especially when the owner of equipment complementary to hers crouched bare inches away.

"Now get another one like that and put it crossways over the first."

"Gotcha." She grabbed a second stick of the same circumference and laid it over the first. "Now bigger ones?"

"Just one. We'll add more later."

She lifted a log that had bark on the rounded side and an exposed honey-colored center on the flat side where someone had split it down the middle. It smelled heavenly, like the inside of the dresser drawer in the bedroom. "What kind of wood is this?"

"Juniper. It's a type of cedar. We have to go up in the mountains a ways to find it, but it's great for burning."

Meg used both hands to hold the wood to her nose and sniff. "Mmm. I wouldn't mind having a hunk of this in my apartment." *Not to mention a hunk like you in there, too, sweet stuff.*

"It smells the best right after you split it. After a while it loses that great smell."

She balanced the log on top of the two smaller branches and glanced at him. "You chopped this wood, didn't you?" When she was so close, she had a chance to admire his dark lashes, which made his eyes seem even more blue. He had a wonderful mouth, too. That didn't always mean a guy was a good kisser, but it was a decent start.

He glanced away, as if having her study him too closely made him uneasy, especially when she was asking questions. "Um, yeah, I chopped it, but it's simple. No real skill involved." He reached for a box of kitchen matches lying on the stone hearth. "Ready to light this fire?"

Was she ever. And in the process, she would peel back the layers of this mysterious, wood-chopping man and expose his honey-colored center, too. Why not? It wasn't as if there was a lot to do in Sonoita, Arizona, once the sun went down.

"I need my gloves off, first."

"Want me to light it?"

"Nope." She pulled off the gloves and took the box of matches. "I built this fire, and I want to be the one to light it." As she slid the box of matches open, she thought about condoms, and hoped to heck he had a stash somewhere, because she was fresh out.

"Strike it away from you, so you won't burn yourself."

Okay, so he was a safety-conscious guy. A safety-conscious guy would have condoms somewhere in this house. She scratched the match over the side of the box. Nothing happened.

"You have to do it faster and harder."

"Oh." She pressed her lips together so she wouldn't laugh. Faster and harder sounded absolutely wonderful. Good thing he understood that. This time she got the match to light with a satisfying *pfft*.

"Now touch it to the paper in several spots. You want to make sure all the wood catches fire, not just a section here and there."

"Always a good idea." She followed his directions to the letter, and soon the small twigs blazed and flames began licking the penis-sized branches. Heat teased her skin, making her long to start stripping off her clothes. What an erotic experience this had turned out to be.

Also, she'd never realized how much you could learn about a man by finding out how he built a fire. If Clint made love with the same patience and precision, she was in for something spectacular. All she had to do was get him to cooperate. And she had the distinct feeling that wouldn't be difficult.

5

CLINT DIDN'T KNOW whether he was coming or going. By rights he should be irritated by a woman who was so obviously helpless in his world. He shouldn't want to get involved with that kind of woman. He liked his sexual partners to be self-sufficient, tough, able to do a man's work if necessary. At least that's what he'd always told himself.

Yet here he was, crouched next to the fireplace with someone who couldn't even strike a match on the first try. And he was turned on. He was so excited, in fact, that he needed to put some distance between him and this great-smelling, sweet-talking, soft and gorgeous female. Giving in to his urges could only bring trouble.

"That should do it for a while." He stood and walked over to the coffee table where José had laid out their place mats and silverware. With the toe of his shoe, he nudged the cushions on the floor a little farther apart and adjusted the place mats accordingly.

Maybe he was reacting to Meg this way because he'd been without for too long. He calculated back to his last encounter. Eighteen months. Time had moved faster than he'd thought. Beverly had wanted marriage and he hadn't been in love, so they'd parted. Hard to believe so much time had passed. He hadn't had the opportunity or inclination again.

"That was fun." Meg got to her feet and gazed at the fire. "It's burning pretty well," she said with obvious pride.

"Uh-huh." And so was he. The urge to kiss her had nearly overwhelmed him while they'd been working on the fire together. She'd looked so damned cute trying to manipulate the wood with those clown-sized gloves. The concentration she'd brought to the job had charmed him.

If she'd been raised in this country, she'd be a top hand. Whatever task she set herself, she'd give it a hundred and ten percent. He couldn't help but admire that. If only he could stop admiring her dynamite body, they could be friends. He'd concentrate on that angle.

The light from outside had faded in the room, leaving only the glow from the fire to outline her drop-dead figure. She created one hell of a silhouette, reminding him of the mud-flap decoration on one of his buddy's trucks. So much for ignoring her body.

"Dinner is served," José called out as he came in with a steaming dish of enchiladas. He set it on the stone hearth.

"Smells delicious," Meg said.

"*Gracias, señorita*." José flashed her a big smile. "I'll be right back with plates and a salad."

Clint had never heard so much Spanish come out of José's mouth before. Meg must be bringing out his inner Ricky Martin.

"I'm starving." Meg eyed the bubbling mixture with longing. "And I'll bet that food is all carbs. I'll need to watch myself."

"You're on a diet?"

"Not by choice. The camera adds pounds, and so to look normal, you have to weigh about ten pounds under your ideal weight. Because I'm on the short side, and kind of busty, I have to be especially careful."

He would say she was more than *kind of busty*. She had the sort of breasts that inspired wet dreams. "Must be tough, watching everything you eat."

"I fall off the wagon all the time, but in New York I belong to a gym, so I can burn those extra calories. I don't have any exercise equipment here."

He could think of another way to burn calories. But he needed to squash those thoughts. He could seriously jeopardize his position here. *Unless she never mentioned it to anyone.*

"Here we are, plates, salad and candles." José bustled back into the room. "I noticed it was getting dark in here."

"We can turn on lights." Clint started toward one of the table lamps next to the sofa.

"Candlelight would be so much nicer," Meg said.

"And *muy bonita*," José added.

Not to mention flat-out seductive. Clint should have turned on the lights earlier, but he'd been too engrossed in Meg to think about such things. Now they had atmosphere, whether he was ready to handle that or not. But he didn't turn on the lights.

José placed two tin candlesticks from Mexico on the coffee table and stuck tapers in them. Clint recognized the candlesticks from years ago, but they'd been in storage for a long time. He was surprised José had candles. Or maybe not so surprised. José had been anticipating this visit for weeks. He'd had plenty of time to buy candles.

"And to drink?" José asked. *"Cerveza?"* he added hopefully.

"Maybe. I don't know what that is," Meg said.

"Beer," Clint said. "Usually José serves Dos Equis with this meal, but you're probably more of a wine drinker."

"Diet Coke."

"Ah, señorita, I beg your pardon. We have no Diet Coke."

"Diet Pepsi?"

José shook his head sadly.

"I could make some more coffee," Clint said.

José glanced at him in alarm. "You made coffee for her? Your normal coffee?"

Meg laughed. "Perked me right up."

"*Señorita*, after a cup of the boss's coffee, you'll be awake for three days. And you'll be lucky if you have enough taste buds left to appreciate my enchiladas. If you want coffee, I'll make it."

"You know what? I'll take some of that *cerveza*, after all. I'll do jumping jacks later on to make up for it."

José's dark gaze swept over her. "You are perfect, *señorita*. No jumping jacks necessary."

"Thank you, José. Trust me, the jumping jacks are absolutely necessary, but I'll worry about that later. Right now I'm ready to eat, drink and make merry."

It was that last part that worried Clint. He could handle a little eating and drinking, but making merry could spell disaster.

"Then sit, sit!" José gestured to the cushions. "I'll bring the *cerveza*."

"Sounds good to me." As José bustled out of the room, Meg walked around the table and sat cross-legged on one of the cushions. "Clint? Care to join me?"

"Right after I put on another log."

"Already?"

"If you let it burn down too low, you have a devil of a time getting it going again."

"So you have to keep it constantly aroused."

Clint thought he might have misunderstood. Surely she hadn't just said what he thought she'd said.

She gave a little gasp of laughter. "Did I really say that out loud?"

He kept his back to her. "Did you say what out loud?" He'd pretend he hadn't heard her.

"Um, nothing. I'm glad you…know so much about tending fires."

"It comes in handy." Heat came at him in waves as he carefully set a fresh log on the blaze. It was nothing compared to the furnace glowing low in his belly.

"I'll bet."

He stood and turned to find her gaze resting firmly on his crotch.

Slowly she lifted the level of her attention until she arrived at his face. "We need to talk."

His pulse galloped like a runaway stallion. "Is that what you have in mind? Talking?"

"To begin with, yes."

"*Cerveza* is here!" José had unearthed a champagne bucket from God-knows where and filled it with ice and four bottles of Dos Equis. He set it, along with two glasses and an opener, in the middle of the coffee table. "Should I serve the enchiladas?"

"We can—" Meg began.

"Yes, please," Clint said. The longer José hung around, the longer Clint could consider what to do about the proposition he suspected was coming once José was out of the picture.

Life sure had a funny way of tripping him up. He never would have guessed that he'd find this kind of chemistry with a television personality from New York City. She might be just as surprised that she craved a hick from the sticks of Arizona. Yet there it was. They wanted each other.

That didn't mean they had to act on it. And while José

made a big production of serving his precious enchiladas and his carefully concocted salad, Clint stared into the fire and came to a difficult decision. He would not take Meg up on the offer she was about to make.

He couldn't risk the possibility that someone would find out. The tabloids would be the least of his problems, although losing his privacy would be a horrible price to pay. But if the word got out, George could retaliate by firing him and that would end any hope of Clint holding onto the Circle W. Clint needed the ranch and Tuck in order to keep training Gabriel, the key to his future earnings.

Meg was almost more temptation than he could stand, but he'd resist, both to preserve his privacy and to maintain his shaky grasp on the ranch. She had goals of her own. She would understand his reasons, so there shouldn't be any bitter feelings.

"The feast is served!" José actually bowed.

Clint was beginning to think José was wasted on a no-frills outfit like the Circle W. He should be running a trendy Mexican restaurant in Tucson or Phoenix, where he could ham it up for the patrons. Of course, José had no start-up money for that.

"I'll leave you to enjoy," José said. "Leave the dishes for me to wash in the morning. I'm taking food down to the bunkhouse and won't be back up tonight."

If that wasn't an engraved invitation to sin, Clint had never heard one. No one would disturb them tonight. He'd be alone for the next twelve hours with a woman most men could only dream about. And he planned to give that golden opportunity a big fat miss.

He turned away from the fire. "Thanks, José. Everything looks great."

"Sure does," Meg said.

"We're honored to have you with us, *señorita*." With another bow, José left the room.

Meg smiled at Clint. "I'm going to guess he doesn't act like that all the time."

"No, he doesn't."

"You're not sitting down. Did I scare you?"

That got to him. "I don't scare easy." He walked over and sat on the cushion that had somehow ended up closer to hers than he remembered. He wondered if she'd moved it when he'd been busy staring at the fire.

"I think we should eat this food while it's hot, don't you?"

"Absolutely." He pulled a cold beer out of the ice bucket, determined to erase any impression that he was a sexual coward. He had to make it clear that he wasn't afraid of her, only the potential consequences. Ignoring the bottle opener, he twisted off the cap. "*Cerveza, señorita?*"

WATCHING CLINT squirm, Meg had to work hard to keep from cracking up. Well, the poor guy was nervous, whether he'd admit it or not, and she understood that. He didn't know that he could trust her to be discreet, for both their sakes.

She understood the stakes better than he did. He might be worried about his privacy, but she had a public image to preserve. She wouldn't take the risk of fooling around unless she could be certain it would remain just between the two of them.

From her first words with Clint, she'd realized how much he valued his quiet life here. That made him the perfect candidate for a secret fling. She hadn't given him the same sense of security, though, and so she was a threat to his future.

"I'd love a *cerveza*," she said. After laying her napkin in her lap, she accepted the cold bottle he held out. A wisp of fog drifted from the open neck of the bottle, and it was slippery from being in the ice bucket. Another phallic symbol. Apparently everything reminded her of sex.

She hadn't poured herself a beer in well over a year, but she still remembered the technique. Tipping her glass, she poured the amber liquid down the side to keep the foam under control. That way it wouldn't spill over onto the table and make a mess. Maybe he'd take that as a small sign that she could be as careful as he was.

When she put the glass down it had exactly the right amount of foam at the top. She glanced over and discovered Clint was concentrating on pouring his own beer with the same amount of precision, as if they were in some kind of contest for beer skills.

She picked up her glass. "Here's to new experiences."

"To new experiences." Touching his glass to hers, he looked into her eyes, as if still trying to decide what she was up to.

She held his gaze as she took her first sip of beer. But when the mellow taste hit her tongue, she closed her eyes in pleasure. Beer was fattening, so she'd denied herself for months. She'd denied herself too many things. Tonight would be different. She'd play hooky from her celebrity role for one night—*if* she could coax her hunky dinner companion to come along for the ride.

When she opened her eyes again, he was staring at her with naked lust. Immediately he looked away and grabbed his fork. "José makes the best enchiladas I've ever tasted." Then he dug in.

"I'm sure he does." She wondered what Clint would do if she stood up and starting peeling off her clothes. She'd bet José's enchiladas, good as they were, would take a back seat.

Oh, yeah, she could seduce him, but he'd be on the verge of panic the whole time, not knowing if his world was about to crash and burn. So she'd assure him first that it wouldn't. Right after she tried the enchiladas.

The first mouthful made her moan with ecstasy. Either sexual arousal heightened all her senses, or José was a culinary genius.

"Good, huh?"

She swallowed and forked up another bite. "The word *good* is too mild for something this incredible."

Clint seemed only too happy with food as a safe topic. "This is the real deal, all right. He starts with his own tortillas and uses extra-rich sour cream and his secret guacamole recipe."

She swallowed her second mouthful. "It's wonderful." But she didn't want him to get too comfortable. Even though they hadn't had their talk, she still needed to keep a steady flame under that fire.

"Glad you like it. José will—"

"Positively orgasmic."

Clint made a strangled sound deep in his throat.

She turned to him, all innocence. "Are you okay? Did something go down the wrong drain?"

"I'm fine." He grabbed his beer and took several swallows.

"I guess it's time we had our talk."

He set down his beer and hopped up from his cushion. "The fire needs another log."

"I want to have sex with you."

He froze in the act of reaching for another piece of wood. Slowly he turned to stare at her. "Did you just say…"

"Yes. I don't have time to be coy. I can tell from your expression that you want me, too."

"I want lots of things. That doesn't mean I allow myself to get stupid. And getting involved with you would be very stupid."

"Not if we both promise to keep our mouths shut."

He was breathing a little faster. "It's not me I'm worried about on that score."

"I realize that. You don't know me very well, yet. But I have as much to lose as you do. I can't afford to let anyone know I got it on with my host at the Circle W."

"I don't see what difference it would make. The tabloids are always printing stuff like that. It creates even more interest in the celebrity, doesn't it?"

God, he was gorgeous. Worth spilling her guts for. "In my case it would be the wrong kind of interest. I'm supposed to come across as the girl-next-door type. Mel's a very conservative guy, and he wouldn't want to co-host with a woman who had a reputation for being easy. A fling with you could backfire on me, big-time."

"But you're out here to find a hot cowboy!"

"Yep, and once he's chosen on the show, I could be seen dating him—briefly. I'm not interested in marriage at this stage in my career, and a torrid affair wouldn't be good for my image. A girl-next-door type doesn't have a lot of latitude, I'm discovering."

He nodded. "Okay, I didn't understand that before, but it makes sense. And the last thing you should consider is taking a chance while you're here."

That's why she felt so safe with him. He wasn't reckless. "It's not a big chance, because I know you wouldn't tell." She pointed to her plate. "As for me, this is the first fattening food I've had in well over a year. I don't drink

beer and I don't eat candy. And my sex life is dead, too—
I've never dared indulge in a wild affair in Manhattan. So
you can see how careful I am."

A hint of a smile touched his mouth. "You must really
want that career of yours."

"I do! I've sacrificed for years to get to this point! And
even though I'm where I dreamed of being, the ratings are
slipping, and now Mona the Vulture is sitting in my seat,
so I could lose it all!" There. She'd revealed fears she'd only
admitted to Jamie. Mona was no girl-next-door type, but
the conniving witch had created that persona for herself
and everyone on the show believed it, especially Mel.

"Sounds kind of scary."

"It is." She took a long swallow of her beer and set the
glass back on the table. "Rumors are flying that I'm not
right for the show. If the ratings are slipping, they have to
blame someone, and they sure as heck won't blame Mel.
He's untouchable."

"I can't believe you're in danger of losing your spot. The
guys in the bunkhouse think you're h—" He coughed and
didn't finish the sentence.

"What?"

"They watch all your shows. Well, except when the reception is lousy. They think you're great."

"Well, sure they started watching when they found out
I was coming to Arizona." In the past few days the ratings
had spiked all over the West, which had pleased the producers. But Meg was afraid she might win the battle and
lose the war to Mona.

"No, they watched before that. And if they couldn't be
around to see it, they had José tape it."

"That's nice to know. But unfortunately, lots of people
have been switching over to *Breakfast with Jack and Jenna.*

The producers hope this Hottest Cowboy promotion will bring them back. That's why they sent me out here. Believe me, it wasn't my idea."

"I thought it was your idea," he said quietly.

"I was kidding when I came up with it. I admitted that I love cowboys, and Mel told me there was no such thing as a real cowboy anymore. I insisted there was, and that maybe I should go find him. It was a joke, but then people started calling in, wanting me to do it. So I had to do it."

"And you don't really want to be here."

She gazed up at him, enjoying the picture of his powerful body surrounded by the glow from the fire. "I didn't want to be here, at first. That was before I met you."

"Except I'm not a real cowboy."

"I'll tell you the truth. I'm a city girl in love with a fantasy. If I found a real cowboy, complete with all those manly rough edges, I probably wouldn't know what to do with him."

"But you think you know what to do with me?"

She looked him over, anticipation making her tremble. "Oh, yeah. I know exactly what to do with you."

6

CLINT WONDERED IF Meg realized she'd given him a challenge any cowboy worth his spurs had to accept. She was a damsel in distress, and she'd asked him to save her. In the larger sense, she needed his help for the Arizona segment of her TV show so that she could save her career.

But her needs included something more immediate and more personal than that. Because of the demands of her career, she was sex-starved, and he was the only man who could relieve that situation. That put a whole different light on the situation.

He no longer saw her as a woman seeking thrills wherever she could find them. Instead she was a slave to the girl-next-door image she was required to maintain. He could remove that burden from her shoulders for the next few hours. Suddenly it seemed like the most noble task in the world.

An hour ago the evening had stretched ahead of him as a long, uncomfortable ordeal. Now it seemed way too short. If she'd been celibate for more than a year, she must be ready to explode.

"So, what do you think, Clint? Care to do me a little favor?" Light from the candles flickered in her eyes.

He'd never been asked by a more beautiful woman.

And she thought he'd be doing *her* a favor. His heart thudded with eagerness.

But he couldn't just drag her off to the bedroom. He'd built one hell of a fire, one that would last several hours. The fireplace was old and the screen couldn't be trusted to hold back the sparks. He couldn't burn down the house that he'd been born in.

"The thing is, I have to…" His voice was hoarse and he stopped to clear his throat. "I can't leave the fire."

"Who said anything about that?"

"I thought…I thought you wanted to go back to the bedroom."

She smiled. "That would be nice, too. But we don't need a bedroom." After getting to her feet, she picked up the cushion she'd been sitting on. "We can improvise."

His brain reeled. She was into spontaneous sex. He'd longed for a woman who was into spontaneous sex. He took a shaky breath. "Guess we could."

"Got condoms?" She sashayed over toward him.

Damn! Were there any left in the box? "Um, yeah. In the—"

"Better go get them. I'll be waiting for you." Then she stood on tiptoe and brushed her lips over his.

For a second he stood there, dazed by that drive-by kiss. He and Meg were really going to do this thing, assuming he wasn't out of condoms. Okay, if he was out, he'd do what she just said. He'd improvise. But condoms would make everything *so* much easier.

But before running off to the bedroom like an errand boy, he needed to take command of the situation. That was especially true if he ended up coming back empty-handed. Her quick peck on the lips lacked the intensity he wanted to establish so they could move past the lack of condoms, if necessary. As she walked by carrying the cushion she intended to plop down in front of the fire, he grabbed her wrist.

She glanced at him in surprise. "I thought you going to get the—"

"First things first." He pulled the cushion out of her arms and dropped it to the floor with a thump. Then he grasped the back of her head and held her steady while he gave her a kiss that would, he hoped, turn the condom issue into a minor problem.

He should have known what to expect, should have been prepared for the rush of pleasure. She'd been telegraphing potency ever since she'd arrived. And the urge to kiss her had been lurking in his subconscious from the moment she'd set her pointed red leather shoes on Circle W property.

But the lust that gripped him as he settled his lips over hers knocked him for a loop. Once he started kissing her, he couldn't seem to stop. She had the most delicious mouth he'd ever explored, and it had very little to do with José's enchiladas. Mostly it had to do with her, a forbidden-fruit-flavored woman if he'd ever tasted one.

She seemed as enthusiastic about the experience as he was. In no time she'd wound both arms around his neck and cuddled that centerfold body right up against his aching groin. The kiss got hotter and wetter, and she began to moan.

Before he knew what he was doing, he'd started unzipping her tight denim pants. The rasp of the zipper must have brought them both around, because they leaped apart as if someone had turned a garden hose on them.

He gasped for breath, and she did the same. If he'd ever reacted this fast to a woman, he had no memory of it.

Maybe this was normal for her. Maybe women from up north had to be more hot-blooded to make up for the freezing weather.

He gulped in air as he backed toward the hallway. "I'll…I'll get the…the…" *Please let me have a full box in that drawer.*

"Good." Breathing hard, she nodded. "That's good."

"You can…" He waved vaguely around the room, his brain too filled with the general idea of sex and the specific issue of condoms to be able to convey details of how they could make themselves comfy.

She nodded again. "I will. I'll set everything up. Don't worry."

He wasn't worried about that, but he was extremely concerned about the contents of his bedside table drawer. He hadn't checked his supplies for eighteen months, hadn't needed to. And he couldn't remember what had been left after Beverly had taken off. It hadn't seemed important then. Now it was an item of more significance than the national debt.

Back in his bedroom he didn't even bother with a light. The box was either there or it wasn't. It was either empty or not. He didn't need a light to find out those critical things.

He wrenched open the drawer. His hand closed over the box. It rattled. Hallelujah! Opening it, he counted one, two, three, four, five. He even checked the expiration date in the dim light coming from the hall. Yeah, he was good to go. If five turned out not to be enough, he'd be so impressed with himself he wouldn't mind running out.

Feeling triumphant, he closed the drawer and started back down the hall. Time to party. His mouth still tingled from that kiss, which had packed more wallop than eight seconds on the back of a bull. To think he'd been ready to turn her down. And him with five unused condoms waiting in the bedside-table drawer.

It seemed that everything had conspired to make this happen tonight. Her sidekick had headed for the bunkhouse, and then all his hands had wimped out on dinner. Fate had tossed them into this house alone tonight, and right now he was a huge supporter of fate.

Moving quickly down the hall, eager to get back to the hot woman waiting in the living room, he heard the distinct sound of rustling clothes. Meg was undressing. With great effort he forced himself to stop and wait until the rustling sounds ended. He needed to remember that she was a performer, a woman with a sense of drama. He didn't want to interfere with that. Hell, he wanted to play to that.

Besides, her clothes probably cost a small fortune. No telling if he'd rip something in his excitement to get them off. Far better to have her do it herself.

As quiet descended, he knew she'd finished. His blood pumped faster than a calf coming out of the roping chute. Until now he hadn't considered the pressure to perform. Of course his fertile brain would deliver the lightning bolt of anxiety right now, when he was about to be tested.

After putting her sexual needs on hold for so long, she'd be expecting fireworks. She'd expect bells to ring and sirens to wail. He'd accomplished that with women in the past, but not under such demanding conditions.

At least she didn't know for sure that he was a cowboy. Thank God for that. If she was cowboy-crazy, as she'd said, then having sex with one would be a fantasy come true. He could never live up to those expectations.

Taking a deep breath, he continued down the hall. First he noticed her clothes laid neatly over the arm of an easy chair. Denim pants and shirt were on the bottom. Then came the white scoop-necked shirt she'd worn underneath the denim. The garments on top made his mouth water—lacy bits of cloth barely big enough to provide decent coverage for those critical areas that claimed all his interest.

He'd like to see her in those undies sometime, as long as he wasn't expected to take them off. He didn't have the dexterity for something that delicate. He could throw a loop over a running calf's hind leg, but he'd never be able to work a woman out of something that lacy and insubstantial without tearing it to bits.

He kept walking, holding the box of condoms in front of him like a gift of diamonds. Right now, they were more precious than diamonds. What a tragedy if that bedside table drawer had come up empty. But it hadn't.

Rounding the chair, he caught his first glimpse of her. In that moment, he knew he would never forget Meg Delancy. He could fall in love with another woman, marry her, father her children and grow old with her. But a picture of Meg lying naked in front of the fire would be with him forever, hovering on the edge of consciousness, reminding him of this night. And no one could ever know. He'd never mention this to anyone.

Unless he became feeble-minded in his old age. If that happened and he started babbling, then chances were he'd babble about this—a red-haired beauty stretched out on three leather sofa cushions, her creamy skin touched by firelight. And she was indeed a true redhead.

She smiled at him. "You found condoms."

"Yes." He'd forgotten the box in his hand, which was an indication of how completely she'd dazzled him. Seconds ago the box had been uppermost in his mind. But she'd blasted everything away but this image of her lying there waiting for him. For *him*. He could barely believe it.

"That's good." Her voice drifted over him like silk.

"You look…amazing." He could spend hours admiring her breasts, let alone her other attributes. Such full breasts, and such a tiny waist. She was breathing fast, which did wonders for the view from above.

"I've worked hard for this body. It's nice to be able to show it off."

"I must be the luckiest guy in the world."

"Not yet. But if you'll take off your clothes, I guarantee you'll get very lucky."

FROM CLINT'S dazed expression, Meg gathered that she'd created the visual impact she'd been going for. Mission accomplished. She hoped the fun she'd had setting this up didn't brand her as a vain girl. But what she'd told him was true. Hours in the gym and a diet with no leeway for indulgence had given her a killer body.

Never had she felt more confident about her body, more ready to take her clothes off for a man. Too bad she had no boyfriend to undress for. Well, tonight she had a man, and maybe she could be forgiven for wanting to show off a little. His response had been extremely gratifying.

However, she didn't want him standing there in a trance forever. Admiration was fine for a little while, but the meter had expired on that phase. Time for some action.

She rose up on one elbow and extended her other hand. "I'll take the box, if you like."

"Oh." He blinked. "Right." He gave it to her.

"Now it's your turn." She nearly licked her lips in anticipation. She'd been admiring his tush ever since following him into the house this afternoon.

Besides the joy of watching him strip down, she'd learn a few things in the process. A guy who rode a desk chair would have a different body from a guy who rode a horse. She had her suspicions about what he was all about, but this getting-naked routine would tell her one way or the other.

He swallowed and unbuttoned the cuffs of his dress shirt. "I'm no movie star." He nudged off his loafers.

"Neither am I." Her pulse rate picked up as he started unfastening the buttons running down the front of his shirt. Such a masculine gesture, those blunt fingers moving steadily down the row of buttons, opening the plackets, opening up to whatever would come next.

"You're nearly a movie star," he said in a voice roughened with urgency. "And you could be one if you wanted to."

She couldn't help reacting to that with a glow of pleasure. It was the exact opposite of what she'd heard growing up. Her parents said they'd warned her against being too ambitious for fear she'd get hurt, but they'd nearly killed her urge to shoot for the moon. "Thank you, Clint. I'm not sure it's true, but thank you."

"It's true. You have...I guess they call it charisma."

Wow. A gorgeous man who was into ego-building. That was a dynamite combo. "I don't know about that, but I hope you're right."

"I am. Although I admit I've never known a celebrity." He pulled his unbuttoned shirt from his slacks and took it off.

"Don't think of me as a celebrity," she murmured. But she'd lost track of the conversation the moment he'd taken off his shirt. All her concentration was on the muscled chest he'd revealed. This was no business consultant.

She'd bet her future in television that those arms could wrestle a steer to the ground or swing an orphaned calf into the saddle for a ride back to the barn. He had a jagged scar—an old one from the pale color of it—on his right shoulder. She decided not to ask him about it now. If he was still in hiding, she didn't need to know. For now, he was giving her more than enough of himself.

"I don't know if I can forget you're a celebrity." He unbuckled his belt.

"I can make you forget." She would make them both forget everything but the joyful search for orgasms.

He shucked his pants. Ah, the forgetting was already starting. When she gazed at the substantial bulge under his gray-knit boxers, she could barely remember her name, let alone what she did for a living.

This was living, lying here waiting for the last piece of clothing to disappear from his rugged body. He pushed his briefs down, and she feasted her eyes on one of nature's sweetest gifts to a woman in her condition—the sight of a fully aroused man.

She sighed, giddy with happiness. "We're going to have such a good time."

"And we're going to take it slow." He sank to his knees beside her. "It's been a while for me, too. I don't want to disappoint you."

She glanced at his super-sized penis. "I doubt that's going to happen."

Bracing his hands on either side of her, he leaned down and nibbled gently at her mouth. "It could if I come too fast."

She slid her fingers through his thick hair and leaned back, bringing him down with her. "You think we're only doing this once?" she whispered against his mouth.

With a groan, he angled his lips over hers and kissed her with soul-searing intensity. She'd never known a man who threw himself headlong into a kiss, as if the kiss alone would bring them to climax. And with each thrust of his tongue, she wondered if it might.

She was still reveling in the sensation of his mouth on hers when he cupped her breast in one large hand, ushering in new delights. She arched upward in ecstasy. At long last, a man was touching her again, and she cherished each caress. His mouth absorbed her soft moans as he molded her like warm clay, massaging her breasts, her belly, her inner thighs…and finally he slipped his hand between her legs.

Shamelessly, she made that part easy for him, lifting as he explored, opening so that his fingers had access. She wanted him to have all the access he required, because she was burning up faster than the logs on the grate.

Yes, there. There. The blunt fingers that had unbuttoned a shirt so efficiently found the way to her wet center with the same precision. He knew the territory well, knew to pause and thoroughly appease the gatekeeper before breaching the inner chamber, knew the rhythm that would make her writhe against the leather cushions.

And when he had her on the brink, he teased her by slowing down. The fire popped and crackled as he drove her into a frenzy with quick thrusts followed by slow caresses. Firm gave way to gentle. He took her up and coaxed her back down again, until at last she broke away from his kiss, panting.

"Please…make me come," she begged in a breathless whisper.

His chuckle was low and sexy. "Just what I wanted to hear."

And before she could draw a breath, he'd slid down until his head was between her thighs. She was too far gone to feel modest. She was too far gone to be shy. She grasped his head and wiggled right into position.

He was still laughing when he kissed her there, which made for a most interesting experience—cool breath and a warm tongue. Then he settled down to business and she lost all sense of time and space. Nothing mattered, nothing counted, but an area no bigger than a bottle cap.

He'd claimed that spot as his own, and it became her whole world. And then her world exploded into waves of pleasure so intense that her strangled cries barely touched on the wonder of it. This single moment justified everything, made all her worries vanish.

He brought her gently back to earth, kissing the inside of her thighs and then her belly, her breasts, her throat, and at last, her mouth.

She gazed up at him, barely able to speak. "Thank... you."

"Seemed like you deserved to start off that way." He looked down at her with tenderness and combed her hair away from her damp forehead with his fingers. "But now I'm interested in what you did with the box I gave you."

"I have...no idea." Once the kissing had started, she'd tossed it somewhere. "I hope it's not in the fire."

"You and me both." He glanced around. "There." After picking up the box, he opened it one-handed and shook out a condom, which landed between her breasts. His eyes sparkled. "What a great pendant that would make."

"An open invitation."

"Especially if you wore it and nothing else." He leaned down and circled her nipple with his tongue.

That was all it took for her to get wound up again. Her

breath caught. "I thought you wanted to put on that little raincoat."

"I will." He sucked gently on her nipple.

"I'm turning into one throbbing nerve ending."

He lifted his head and switched to her other breast. "Good." Nuzzling and licking, he made her breasts quiver and her nipples tighten.

In the process he created havoc with her pulse rate. An ache grew inside her, one that needed more than another climax. This was the primitive kind of ache, the urge that demanded penetration. She'd never felt it quite this strongly before.

She closed her eyes and pictured the glory of his penis. She wanted to experience that glory. "If you don't put that condom on, I'm going to do it for you. And I'm not very good at it."

He gave her breast one last swipe with his tongue. "Fortunately, I am." Then he picked up the packet with his teeth and sat back on the edge of the cushion to tear it open.

She lifted her head so she could watch. True to his word, he was quick with a condom. She was reminded of a rodeo cowboy tying the legs of a steer with a pigging string and holding up his hands for time. She almost expected Clint to do that once the condom was in place.

"You are fast," she said when he glanced up to find her checking him out.

His smile was filled with male confidence as he moved between her thighs, poised for his first thrust. "I've been told it's not nice to keep a lady waiting. Too much time spent on that latex is time wasted."

"You've been told right. I hate waiting."

"And here I am." He probed her moist center, finding entry, sliding in a fraction.

"That's it." She wrapped her arms around his waist and lifted her hips in his direction. "Come on and give me a ride, cowboy."

His eyes widened. "I'm not—"

"Never mind." The words had slipped out because she was so sure, so very sure, that he was, indeed, a cowboy.

"Meg, I—"

Damn. She hadn't meant to start a discussion. "I know what. Why don't you see if you can make me forget I ever said that?"

"Sounds like a plan." He pushed deep.

Exactly. Exactly that. She hadn't known how much she'd craved having him inside her until he was there, stroking with steady intent. In seconds, she was oblivious to anything but the breathless climb to another shattering orgasm. He might be a cowboy. He might not. In the midst of such delirious joy, she didn't care.

7

CLINT HAD TAKEN hold of a whirlwind. Here he was, in the male-dominant position, the one that supposedly guaranteed the most control of this event, and he had no control whatsoever. Oh, he could hold back his orgasm. That wasn't as difficult as he had thought it would be when he'd first entered her and felt her warmth pulsing around him.

But his emotions were totally out of control. As he looked into those gorgeous brown eyes, he wanted to say things to her—significant things that had no business being part of this experience.

He wanted to tell her that he felt connected to another human being for the first time in his life. Sex was about satisfaction, but this...this touched him on a different level. He hadn't expected that.

As he thrust rhythmically, he was acutely aware of her, as if he'd climbed inside her mind at the same moment he'd penetrated her body. He swore he could tell what she was thinking, and that she was as rattled by this emotional jolt as he was.

"Meg." Saying her name was all he could allow himself. But he put a world of feeling into that one syllable.

"I'm here."

"I know. Me, too." Maybe that was it. They were both

completely *there*. His every sense was alert. His ears hummed with the crackle of the fire and the sound of her breath. His nose filled with the scent of wood smoke and the tang of arousal. His mouth savored the taste of her kisses. And crowning each of those sensations was the unbelievable pleasure he felt each time he buried his penis deep in her quivering vagina.

Her smile trembled. "So perfect."

She'd said more than he'd dared. "Yes." His orgasm moved closer with sweet inevitability. There was no strain to bring it on, no pressure to hold it back. He would come, and so would she. And the moment would be effortless.

"This is like...dancing."

With someone I've known all my life. He nodded, because he couldn't tell her that.

Without conscious thought he pumped faster, and she flowed into the new rhythm without hesitation. He'd never believed that two people could truly feel as if they had become one. He'd chalked that up to some poet's fantasy.

With Meg, it was reality.

"Clint...." She turned his name, a name that had always seemed to have such hard edges, into a gentle caress.

"Almost there." But he didn't really need to speak at all. They both knew exactly where they were, hovering on the brink of a mutual climax with the power to change what they believed about themselves, what they thought about each other.

Maybe if he'd known this could happen, he'd have found the strength to refuse her. Discovering something so amazing and knowing it couldn't last was a cruel joke. But he couldn't stop the avalanche now.

"Hang on," he murmured.

"As tight as I can." Her eyes grew bright.

"Here we go." Closing his eyes would be some protection, but he couldn't do it. Having gone this far, he wanted everything.

Her pupils widened and she dug her fingers into his back. And she didn't look away.

Blood rushed in his ears as the first wave crashed over him. He kept going, holding her gaze as fiercely as she held his, matching her cry for cry. He watched her through each surge, watched the flush of orgasm glide up over her breasts, her throat, her face as he poured himself into her with a force that left him breathless.

He held her gaze as the quivering slowly subsided and they both struggled to breathe. He would not take the cowardly way out and look away. Whatever had happened between them, he would have the courage to face it.

For a long while her eyes reflected only wonder. Then her expression changed, and he saw the one emotion he didn't want there—regret.

He leaned down and kissed her mouth, her cheeks, her forehead. "Hey, none of that."

"I didn't know. I had no idea."

"Neither of us knew." He looked into her eyes again. "We only planned on having a little fun."

"It was more than that."

"Uh-huh."

She was silent for several long moments. "Now what?"

"You already know the answer." He smiled at her, touched that she even had doubts about what came next. "You'll go on with your life and I'll go on with mine. That was the deal before, and it's still the deal."

She cupped his face in her hands. "Can you stand it?"

"Yes. Because that's the way it has to be. I don't want your life, and you don't want mine." He landed a kiss on the tip of her nose. "Crummy TV reception in Sonoita, remember?"

"You're a cowboy, aren't you?"

He kissed his way along her jawline and gave a little tug on her earlobe. "I don't know what being a cowboy has to do with the price of jalapeños."

"That's why you wouldn't want my life. You need the wide-open spaces."

He lifted his head to gaze down at her. Continuing to play games made no sense anymore. "Yeah, I suppose I'm a cowboy."

"I knew it." She ran her hands along his shoulders. "You have too many muscles to be a business consultant. And I'll bet you got this scar doing something cowboyish."

"Something dumbish. Got crosswise of a very irritated Brahma. I barely made it under the barbed-wire fence in time. The bull didn't get me, but the fence did."

She traced the uneven line of the scar. "Why didn't you want me to know you were a cowboy?"

"I'm sure you can figure that one out, too."

"You didn't want to be on TV?"

"Bingo."

She cradled his face again and studied him earnestly. "You would be awesome on TV."

"Don't even go there, pretty girl. I've told you the truth, and you have to promise not to use it against me."

She opened her mouth, as if to argue with him.

"No." He gave her a quick, hard kiss, as if that would put the lid on the matter. He hoped to hell it would. This discussion had been a good thing, reminding him of how far apart they were, lessening the effect of the moment they'd just shared. "And now that we have that settled, we're back to figuring out our next move."

She looked into his eyes for several long seconds. "Would it be better if I spent the rest of the night in my own room?"

"I suppose that would be the sensible thing."

"Then I'll do that." Taking a deep breath, she gave him a brave smile. "Let me up and I'll be on my way."

He didn't move. "You didn't ask me if I wanted to be sensible."

"Oh." The brave smile wavered as she searched his expression. "You don't?"

"No. But that's just me. You get a vote, too. If you want to play it safe, I wouldn't blame you a bit. I'll let you go and promise not to sneak into your bed during the night to try to change your mind."

Her smile returned. "Maybe I'd be the one sneaking into your bed. I have to say if we make a pact to keep our hands to ourselves from now on, it's going to be a very long night."

"That would be true." He couldn't imagine how he'd make it, knowing she was in a room right down the hall. "So what do you think?"

"I think…" She paused.

Impatient though he was for her final verdict, he reminded himself that dramatic pauses were likely her stock-in-trade. He didn't want to rush her when he had a fair idea what her decision would be.

"I think we should keep doing this."

His triumph was bittersweet. Short-term pleasure, long-term heartache. The key to surviving would be to establish a playful mood and avoid the heavy stuff. "Define what you mean by *keep doing this*. Do you mean lying here in front of the fire having a conversation?"

She reached down and pinched his butt. "I mean having a mutual-orgasm fest, and you know it."

"Just wanted to be clear." Looked like she'd taken his cue to keep things light, just as she'd kept up with him perfectly as they'd roared together to a climax. They were beautifully matched. Dammit.

"Then let me be even more clear. I want to have a super-duper boinkathon. I want to keep doing it 'til the cows come home."

He pretended to think about that. "That could be a really long event, because we don't have any more cows on the Circle W. You could be waiting quite a while for one to wander into the barn."

"I knew that." She grinned at him. "It's all part of my plan to enslave your virile body."

"In that case, maybe we'd better eat more of José's enchiladas, to keep up our strength."

"Naked?"

He winked at her. "Absolutely."

CLINT INSISTED on heating up the enchiladas, even though Meg would have been happy to eat them at room temperature. She usually had meals on the run, and she rarely ate anything exciting, so she'd given up worrying about the quality of her food. Because Clint had José, he was spoiled rotten. She wondered what it would be like to live here and eat José's cooking all the time. She'd turn into a hippo, no doubt, unless she worked off the calories having lots of sex.

After Clint poked at the fire until he seemed convinced that no sparks would escape while they were gone, he invited her into the kitchen while he heated up the food. She carried their glasses of beer while he brought the pan of enchiladas.

She imagined that heating up the enchiladas wouldn't take more than a few minutes in the microwave. Then they could return to their cozy spot in the living room. But to her amazement, Clint turned on the oven and stuck the pan inside.

"Aren't you going to nuke them?" She glanced around the kitchen to locate the appliance she couldn't live without. Well, not counting the vibrator in her bedroom, of course.

"José doesn't believe in them." Clint closed the oven door and picked up the beer she'd set on the counter for him.

She leaned against the counter, which was tiled in the same bright pattern as the bathroom counter. "Then I'll make an educated guess that you don't have a month's supply of frozen dinners in the freezer." As she did.

"That would be a good guess." He picked up his beer, took a swallow and grimaced. "This is both warm and flat." He poured it down the sink. "Yours must be the same." He reached for the glass she was holding.

"No, mine's just fine!" She held it away from him. Assuming the Circle W was on a tight budget, she wasn't about to waste whatever was given to her.

"Can't be fine. Yours sat out there as long as mine did." He pinned her to the counter with his hips and got his hand around the top of her glass. "Let me get rid of it and pour you a new one."

"No." She tightened her grip on the glass, but wiggled her hips and cupped his tush with her free hand. "However, I like your method of intimidation a lot."

"You're using your feminine wiles on me so I won't take your beer, aren't you?"

"Maybe. And judging from the response I'm getting,

my wiles are working great. I think you've almost forgotten about the beer."

"Have not." He wrapped his other arm around her waist and started tickling her.

She squirmed, protesting even as she giggled helplessly. "No fair! I'm going to pinch you if you don't stop!"

"Go ahead. I like it when you pinch me. It gets me hot." He continued to tickle her as he tried to pry the beer loose. "Ouch! That was a serious pinch!"

"Warned you!" She couldn't remember when she'd last wrestled with a naked man. She was having way too much fun. "I'll stop pinching you when you stop tickling me. And let go of my beer, dammit!"

"I'm gonna get your beer whether you like it or not." He was breathing hard. "Pinch away."

"You asked for it." But when she tried for a better grip on his fanny, he managed to get the beer glass away from her. As she let go, he jerked the glass toward him and splattered the contents down her front and his.

The cool liquid made her skin tingle and her nipples tighten. "Whoo-hoo! I don't know what you're talking about! That beer is definitely not warm!"

He put down the glass, stood back and surveyed the beer dripping from her breasts. "If it wasn't warm before, but I'll bet it is now. You're a mess. Allow me to take care of that for you." He swooped down to lap the beer from her skin.

She started laughing. "Hey, I thought you didn't like warm beer."

"I guess it's all in the delivery system." He continued to clean her with broad swipes of his tongue. "I'd drink lighter fluid if it came packaged like this."

Watching him lick her with such enthusiasm was turn-

ing her on, plus it gave her an outstanding idea. The beer
had anointed him, too, landing on a certain projecting part
of his anatomy. Still, she didn't think he was wet enough
to justify what she had in mind.

Taking the glass from the counter, she tapped him on
the shoulder. "Uh, Clint?"

"What?" He lifted his head.

"There's some beer left in the glass. Want me to pour
it out?"

His eyes sparkled with lust. "Yeah. Pour it, baby. I need
a good excuse to keep this up a while longer. Maybe it'll
drip farther down this time."

She could imagine what fun that might be, but she had
a different concept in mind. "Okay." Instead of pouring it
on herself, she tilted the glass so the stream of beer cas-
caded over his penis on its way to the floor. "Whoops.
Missed."

"Doesn't matter." He leaned toward her breasts again.
"I can make do with whatever is left."

"No, no. Let me handle this." Dropping to her knees,
she ran her tongue slowly around the tip of his penis
where droplets of beer had gathered.

He groaned. "Okay, I get it."

"Hold still and you just might." She glanced up at him.
"To think you poured your warm beer down the drain."

"I don't know what I was thinking."

"Me, either." And she began to lick him clean. She did
a complete, detail-oriented job, and to make certain that
she got all the beer off, she drew him deep into her mouth
and sucked vigorously. One couldn't be too thorough
when cleaning up one's messes.

He hung onto the counter and moaned. Then he began
to shake. "Meg, you need to…stop."

She didn't feel like it. Having him completely in her power was exhilarating and stopping wasn't an option she wanted to consider. Besides, his request had sounded on the halfhearted side. Chances were he didn't mean it.

On that assumption, she kept going. If he wanted her to stop, he'd ask again. Surprise, surprise, he didn't. Instead his groans became louder and his shudders more intense. She had him now.

When he came, she felt a personal sense of victory. Until now he'd been the one in charge of orgasms. Maybe he'd been following some Code of the West in that regard, but this kitchen event had restored some balance to their interaction. Meg thought that was a good thing considering how off-balance she'd felt since the moment they'd met.

CLINT DAMNED NEAR burned the enchiladas, but it was worth it. How he'd explain the condition of the kitchen to José was something he'd have to work out later. He and Meg washed the floor with damp paper towels, but he was so fascinated by the way her breasts jiggled while she scrubbed that he doubted he'd got all the beer off the tiles.

And the enchilada pan would require a heavy soaking because he'd left it in the oven too long. Other things going on. Oh, yeah. Incredible things.

Once they were back in the living room, Clint moved the cushions over behind the table again. This time he made sure they were as close together as possible. When they sat down cross-legged, she parked her knee on top of his, which was exactly the way he liked it.

The fire had burned down to a bed of glowing embers, and he decided not to build it up. After they ate he planned to suggest they try out the comforts of an actual bed. The thought of Meg stretched out on his mattress took away all interest in food, but he didn't want to deprive her of José's cooking when she obviously didn't allow herself to eat like this very often.

She dished the enchiladas and salad while he opened two more bottles of beer. "I've never eaten dinner naked," she said.

"That makes two of us." But he could get used to it. Without clothes, they were just two people enjoying each other's company, each other's bodies. He could forget, sort of, that she was famous and he was…not.

She ate with gusto, obviously loving every bite. Then she paused, her fork in the air. "This is so good. Do you have meals like this all the time?"

"We have a lot of good chow, if that's what you mean. Not always Mexican, either." He was having too much fun looking at her to concentrate on his food. "José makes all sorts of stuff. One Christmas he cooked Beef Wellington. He whips up a mean spaghetti sauce, too."

She moaned. "Spaghetti. I can only dream about spaghetti."

"I don't get it." He surveyed her incredible body. "You look like you could eat anything you wanted."

"That's what people always say to me, but inside this skinny body is a fat person waiting to get out, hoping I'll gobble up the package of Chips Ahoy sitting in my freezer and top that off with a gallon of Sticky Chewy Chocolate ice cream."

Clint took a swallow of his beer. "It's none of my business, but are you sure this job is worth starving yourself and going without sex?"

"It's what I've wanted my whole life—to be in front of the camera—and now I'm finally there." She glanced at him. "There's no such thing as a free lunch, you know. Or a nonfattening one."

"I know, but are you sure you're having a good time, considering all you're sacrificing?"

She paused, as if giving the question serious thought. "I have a good time when I'm on the air. I really do love being on camera, joking around with Mel and interviewing guests. So yes, it's worth it. There's nothing quite like the moment when we go live."

"Then I guess you're in the right place." While talking about her work, she seemed to take on the charisma of a celebrity, even though she was sitting here buck-naked in his living room.

"I think I am, too," she said. "But I hardly ever spend time wondering about it. I'm too busy doing it. If I'm not on the show, I'm making appearances or I'm at the gym or the salon." She combed her fingers through her hair. "I'll bet at this moment I don't look like a woman who spends hours at a beauty salon."

"Yes, you do." He loved the tousled look of her, the kissed and thoroughly loved look of her. He reached over and wrapped a lock of her silky hair around his finger. "You muss up real good."

She grinned at him. "Sweet of you to say that. And it's fun to forget being polished, even for one night. Sometimes the maintenance angle gets to me. I've fantasized going off to a desert island for a week so I could have seven days of not caring about hair, nails and makeup."

"You might not like it. I mean, aren't you used to having everything perfect?"

"Yes, but that doesn't mean I *need* to have everything perfect."

He was inclined to believe her. From the moment she'd walked into the living room tonight, she'd shown no interest in finding a mirror so she could primp. That impressed him.

"I love performing," she said, "but I could do without the constant work to keep moderately presentable."

"I'd say you hit a higher standard than moderately presentable."

"Thanks." She smiled. "I try."

"You succeed." But listening to her, he couldn't figure out her reasons for staying in this career. Near as he could tell, she had five hours of fun per week, tops.

She picked up her glass of beer and took a sip. "How about you? I'll bet there are disadvantages to your job, too. Don't you have to shovel smelly horse poop?"

He laughed. "Yes, ma'am, I do."

"You sounded exactly like a cowboy when you said that." Her eyes twinkled. "Tomorrow will you put on your cowboy duds for me?"

"I don't know." He grew wary. "Depends on where Jamie is pointing that camera."

She put down her beer and reached over to stroke his cheek. "I can't believe it would be that horrible for you. Most people think it's fun."

"Not me. If there's the slightest chance you'll try to rope me into this production of yours, then you'll never see me in jeans and boots."

She cupped his face in both hands. "I'd love to see you in jeans and boots. I wasn't kidding about my cowboy fantasy."

He brought her hands to his mouth and placed a string of kisses there. "But you said you wouldn't know what to do with a real cowboy."

"I didn't think I did." Her voice grew husky. "But you've changed my mind."

He looked into her eyes and desire hit him hard, heating his skin, his blood, his brain. "I didn't think I'd know what to do with a TV star, either."

"But you do."

"So far, so good." And he'd be fine as long as he didn't let himself get lassoed and hog-tied by Meg's charm.

"So far, *very* good," she murmured.

He wanted her so much he had to fight not to grab her. "Had enough of José's cooking for a while?"

"If that's an invitation to visit your bedroom, I accept."

His heart beat loud and fast. "It was a solid-gold, engraved invitation."

She stood and held out her hand. "Then let's go get it on, cowboy."

8

"So I END up in your bedroom, after all." She let go of his hand and surveyed the space, admiring the sturdy four-poster and matching mahogany dresser. If she'd been given this room to start with, she would have known instantly that a cowboy lived here.

There were framed pen-and-ink drawings of cowboys on the walls, for one thing, and a brown felt cowboy hat lay brim-side-up on top of the dresser. But the dead giveaway was a pair of worn boots sitting next to a ladder-back chair in the corner.

Crossing to the chair, she picked up the boots. "Yours, I presume?"

"Mine." He watched her from the doorway of the bedroom. "That's sort of kinky, seeing a naked lady holding my boots."

"Want me to put them on?"

"I don't want you to put anything on. I like you exactly the way you are."

"That's nice to hear." She studied the scuffed boots and inhaled the scent of leather, dust and horse sweat. Funny what a thrill she got from knowing that Clint wore these boots while doing his cowboy thing. Mel had scoffed at the idea that there were any real cowboys left, but she believed she'd stumbled upon one.

"I hate to disappoint you, but I don't wear them to bed."

She set down the boots and smiled at him. "Aw, shucks. How's a girl supposed to fulfill her fantasies?" She glanced across the room toward the hat lying on the dresser and lifted her eyebrows.

He laughed. "No, I'm not wearing my hat to bed, either."

"You're no fun." But she was only teasing him. She didn't need props to fire her imagination. Gazing at him standing there in all his lean-hipped glory was fantasy enough for her.

"If a cowboy experience is what you crave, maybe instead of the bedroom we should head on down to the barn and do it on a hay bale, with the horses looking on."

The idea kicked up her pulse a notch. "Are you serious?"

"Not really. The barn's close to the bunkhouse, and neither one of us can take that kind of risk. But I like the way your eyes lit up when I suggested it."

"Because it sounded pretty darned exciting! But you're right. We can't take the chance that someone would be out wandering around." But now that he'd mentioned it, the image of having sex in the barn had a permanent spot in her mind.

Horses on the loose scared her. Her mom had taken her as a rambunctious four year old to a parade in New York City, and she'd accidentally darted in front of a giant police horse. Although she'd only been knocked to the ground, the image of that horse looming over her still gave her nightmares. But these horses would all be safely put away in stalls.

"Have you ever had sex in the barn before?" she asked.

"Not for a long time."

"But you have done it?" She was fascinated by the concept.

"Sure. When you grow up out in the country, it's a fairly safe place to go make out with a girl, and the horses won't tell on you. I used to keep a condom stuck in a little space between two boards."

"Ingenious."

"I thought so until one night when I reached for it, it was gone. What a nightmare."

For his girlfriend, too, she thought. "I can imagine. All worked up and no place to go."

"*That* wasn't a problem—we just switched to plan B. The real nightmare was that I was afraid it had fallen on the floor and a horse had swallowed it, and I didn't know what that might do to its digestive system. Horses have delicate stomachs."

"So what happened?"

"My dad let me sweat for days until finally he told me he'd found it, and that I was damned lucky a horse hadn't found it first. After that I carried them in my wallet, like everybody else."

"And what was plan B?"

His smile grew lazy and sensuous. "Oh, I'll bet you can guess."

"I suppose so." To think that as a teenager, he'd known all about oral sex. Meg envied every country girl who had been privy to a literal roll in the hay with Clint. The idea seemed so much more exotic than fondling each other in the back row of a movie theater. Her dates hadn't been very adept at plan B.

"Meg, stop looking like that. I can't take you out to the barn, and you know it."

"You're right. But now I'll always want to."

"Yeah, well…" He didn't finish the sentence.

He didn't have to finish it. She knew what he hadn't said, that she'd chosen a life that didn't leave room for sexual adventures in barns.

As if to change the subject, he walked over to an archway, reached inside the darkened space and flipped on a light. "Bathroom's in here, by the way."

She looked through the archway and glimpsed a large shower stall that ran across the entire back wall. It was covered in the same bright flower pattern as the rest of the tiled surfaces in the house. Instead of being blocked by a shower curtain, the space was partially enclosed by a tiled wall about five feet high.

"Great shower." She walked toward the arched doorway for a closer look.

"Thanks. I put it in last year. Got sick of squashing myself into the tiny one that used to be there, so I made it bigger."

"You did this yourself?" She stepped into the bathroom so she could inspect the tiling job.

"Yeah." He followed her in. "I work cheaper than anyone I know."

"I'm impressed with how professional it looks." She ran her hand down the smooth tile. "I can barely change a lightbulb."

"I like working with my hands." His voice was husky.

"I know." She met his gaze and smiled. "You have real talent in that area."

His blue eyes grew hot. "Glad you think so, because I have the urge to do some work with my hands right now."

"Hold that thought." Slowly she turned back to the shower, her imagination set on high. She might not be able to have sex in the barn with Clint, but she could have sex in the shower that he'd created. That was almost as good.

"Come on in and bring a condom." She stepped over the tiled edge of the shower and reached for a chrome handle marked with an *H*. "We're going to make a memory."

EVEN THOUGH Clint joined Meg in the shower, even though he was eager to get his hands on her again, he knew he'd live to regret it. No one had used this shower except him, and once he'd had sex with her in it, he'd never be able to wash up here without thinking about her body, her kiss, her scent.

Nevertheless, he wasn't going to give up the chance, just as he hadn't been willing to give up anything she'd offered from the moment she'd arrived. But when she left the ranch, her vibrant memory would be everywhere, haunting him for as long as he stayed in this house.

He wouldn't think about that now.

Instead he laid the condom packet in the soap dish, adjusted the water temperature and stepped under the warm spray. She wrapped her arms around him and wiggled in close, allowing the water to cascade over her head and soak her hair. With him, she seemed to have no concern about her looks.

As he gathered her in and dipped his head to kiss her wet mouth, he wondered if her unconcern was a compliment because she felt at ease with him. Or maybe she didn't care enough to be worried about her appearance.

It didn't matter. He'd always dreamed of a woman who would leap into experiences without first spending a half hour in front of a mirror. Meg obviously had enough self-confidence to do that.

He'd never kissed a woman while standing smack-dab in the middle of the shower, and he liked it. The warm water tapped on his skin with a gentle massage, and the kiss was wet and warm.

The water skimmed over and between their bodies, lubricating the tiny spaces between them so they could slide against each other like oiled machinery. He rubbed every inch of her he could reach, loving the way his hand slipped over her skin without resistance, but with enough friction to make her moan against his mouth.

Then her touch joined the dance of water over his skin. Her liquid caress moved over his shoulders, down his back, following the curve of his spine. When she cupped his butt and squeezed gently, his penis twitched and his balls tightened. She seemed to know exactly what he needed next, bringing both hands around, grasping gently, stroking and fondling as the water sluiced over his belly and between his legs.

He could come like this in no time at all, but he wanted to hold off. He knew something about this shower that she might not have noticed. Easing away from her kiss, he backed out of reach.

"More." Dark lashes spiked with water framed her smoldering gaze. Her hair was plastered to her head and her makeup was completely gone. She looked fantastic. "Come back here," she murmured.

"Not yet." He reached up and detached the shower head from its holder.

She glanced at it. "Massage?"

"Uh-huh." He played the fine spray over her aroused nipples. "Want to play?"

"Sure." She licked her lips, and her breath came faster.

"Ever used one?"

"Mmm."

He should have guessed she had, in her sex-deprived state. "Ever had someone else do it?"

She shook her head.

"Good. New experience. Maybe you'd better lean against the wall."

She nodded and backed up to the tile.

As if he were spray-painting a statue, he swept the shower head slowly back and forth. He covered her breasts, fascinated by the pattern of the water pouring over that beautiful landscape. "Turn the dial," he murmured. "Find out what feels the best."

She grasped the outer rim of the shower head and twisted. The fine spray became a pulsing beat of water against her rosy skin. Closing her eyes, she moaned softly. "That's good."

"Then here we go." He moved the spray down, anticipation making him hard and ready. He wondered if he could come simply because he knew she was about to.

At first he waved the spray across the tops of her thighs, teasing her. "Talk to me. Tell me what to do."

Her eyes fluttered open and she drew in a ragged breath. "Are you a good shot?"

"Some say I am."

"Then aim that thing, pardner. Hit the target."

He grinned. "Done." He pointed the shower head and watched her gasp and arch into the pulsing jets.

"Harder," she whispered.

He turned up the pressure and felt as if he'd twisted some internal dial on his own lust. The faster the water beat against her, the more he wanted to replace that pulsing spray with his aching penis. But he knew better than to interrupt at a moment like this. A wise man finished what he'd started.

He nudged the spray closer, and she began to quiver. Then, with a deep groan, she grasped the shower head in both hands and took exactly what she needed. That moment of complete abandon would be seared into his brain forever, along with her cries and the staccato beat of the water caressing her to climax.

She was the woman he'd waited a lifetime to find—open about her needs, unself-consciously sexual, eager for adventure. The combination made her wildly attractive, inspiring a lust he could barely control.

When at last she sagged against the tile and released her grip, he let the shower head dangle free, shut off the water and gathered her quaking body close. His raging body demanded satisfaction, and he wasn't ready to take a chance on a slippery shower stall. Mattress time.

After lifting her into his arms, he carried her out of the shower, through the archway and over to his bed.

She gazed up at him. "We're all wet. We'll soak your bed."

"I don't care." He plopped her down on his quilted bedspread, grabbed a condom from the box he'd left on the nightstand and put it on. "I can't wait until we're dry." Then he climbed onto the bed. "Don't expect technique."

She still seemed dazed by her recent orgasm. "What…should I expect?"

"Basic sex. And excellent aim." He thrust deep and began to pump.

Her sigh was rich with pleasure. "Good."

Sad to say, he wasn't concerned about that. Later he would concentrate on her, but he was too far gone to do anything but gaze down at her flushed face as he stroked. *Ah, like that. Yes. And faster.* The bed squeaked. The headboard hit the wall. So close…. *There.*

As he erupted, he was amazed to feel her contractions as she followed him over the edge. Fast and furious worked for her, too. That was good news. He'd focus on that and forget that there was any bad news at all.

THROUGHOUT the rest of the night, Meg shoved away thoughts of morning. She couldn't be concerned about morning when she was having the best sex of her entire life. Her sense of responsibility would alert her when the end of this outstanding experience was approaching.

She didn't count on her sense of responsibility taking a powder for the night. When her cell phone rang in her bedroom, she didn't hear it. She'd fallen into the deepest sleep she'd known in years. She was aware of nothing at all until Clint shook her gently, and she opened her eyes to find him holding her phone and looking worried.

"Your phone rang. I didn't dare answer it, but I'm afraid we...overslept."

He might as well have hit her in the chest with a sledgehammer. She bounded from the bed and grabbed the phone to retrieve Jamie's message. He sounded frantic. She speed-dialed his cell. "Jamie! Hi!" Searching wildly for a clock, she found one on the dresser. Past seven.

"Where are you?" Jamie sounded agitated, as well he should. They had twenty-five minutes before they had to be on the bird. That was barely enough prep time.

"I'm on my way." Cell phone to her ear, she ran naked into her bedroom. "Get the foreman, what's-his-name, and make sure he's ready to be interviewed."

"He's been ready for an hour. I thought you'd be here by now. We need to—"

"I'll be right there." She punched the button to hang up the phone and tossed it on her still-made bed.

"What can I do?" Clint asked from the doorway.

"Better stay out of my way." She threw open the closet door and grabbed the first thing she found, a black fringed jacket and black cropped pants. The pants were creased. "Can you iron?"

"Yes."

"Here." She threw the pants in his direction and rummaged in a drawer for underwear. By the time she barreled through the door headed for the bathroom across the hall, he'd disappeared with her pants. "Thanks!" she called after him.

Her first glimpse in the mirror made her leap back in shock. Her hair stuck out like the bristles of an old paint brush, and her chin was deep pink from whisker burn. And she had ten minutes to pull herself together.

No time for a shower, no time to shampoo her hair. She knelt down by the bathtub, turned on the faucet and stuck her head underneath. Then she dripped her way back to the sink, snatching a towel from the rack on the way.

With the towel around her shoulders, she yanked a comb through her hair and swore loudly. This couldn't be happening. She should have asked Clint to set an alarm, but she'd never overslept before. *Never.* She was so used to waking up early five days a week that she did it automatically on Saturday and Sunday, too. But not today.

After pulling her blow dryer out of the cosmetic case, she held the plug and searched for an outlet. There had to be an outlet. No outlet. She whirled in a circle, fighting hysteria. "Clint! Help!"

He came running. "What? What's the matter?"

"No outlet! I have to dry my—"

"Right here." He took the plug and pushed it into an outlet attached to the light beside the mirror.

"If that isn't the craziest place for it!" She snapped the blower on high.

He shrugged and started back down the hall.

She hadn't even thanked him. Turning off the dryer, she yelled out "Thanks!" but got no response. She didn't have time to worry about whether she'd hurt his feelings or not. Her entire career hung in the balance.

By the time he came back holding her pressed slacks, she'd dried and sprayed her hair into submission. It still looked bad, but not as bad. "Thank you," she said as he hung the slacks gently over a towel rack. Then she started smoothing makeup over her whisker-burned chin.

"Anything else?"

"I guess not, unless you can get me a new face."

"What's wrong with yours?"

"Whisker burn." She hadn't meant it to be an accusation, but it sounded like that, anyway. "It's not your fault," she added, dabbing more coverup on the area.

"I know it isn't," he said quietly. "This is your job, not mine."

"That's for sure." She sighed and put down the tube of coverup. Maybe powder would take care of the rest.

"If there's nothing more I can do, I'll get dressed and go down to the bunkhouse."

"Clint, I'm sorry to be so abrupt, but I—"

"Don't worry about it." Then he was gone.

Obviously he was unhappy with her, but she couldn't deal with that now. Hell, she was unhappy with herself. But she couldn't indulge in self-recrimination, either. All that mattered was getting down to the bunkhouse in time.

9

AFTER QUICKLY shaving off the stubble that had caused Meg so much anxiety, Clint hesitated only a moment before pulling on his jeans. Once he got to the bunkhouse he'd tell the guys that his original plan had been scrapped. Trouble was, he had no plan to put in its place.

A few hours ago he'd been in heaven, and now he was in hell. The carefree woman he'd spent the night with had morphed into a career-driven maniac. He didn't blame her for it—in a few minutes she would appear before millions of her fans and she didn't feel ready. That could throw anyone into a frenzy.

But the transformation had been a slap of cold reality, reminding him that no matter how perfect she'd seemed while she'd lain naked and willing in his arms, she was not the woman for him. Never had been, never would be. Just as well. He didn't need a woman in his life. He had his hands full worrying about the future of the Circle W.

Even so, he mourned the loss of that special feeling he and Meg had shared. For two people to fall into sync so quickly had to be unusual. No matter how many times he'd told himself the feeling couldn't last, he hadn't been prepared for it to end like this. He felt emotionally cut off, amputated from all that was warm and sweet.

Now he had to go down to the bunkhouse and act as if

nothing had happened up here last night. That could have been easier if he and Meg had cooked up a story about how they'd passed the evening. They hadn't had time for that.

Still, before he left the house he ought to do a few things to cover their tracks. She was still in the bathroom putting on her war paint when he went into her bedroom and tossed back the covers on the bed she'd never slept in. After rumpling the sheets, he smacked his fist into the pillow, denting it as if she'd put her head there all night.

From there he went into the living room, where the scent of wood smoke brought back potent memories. Her clothes lay across the back of the easy chair and his clothes were crumpled haphazardly on the floor. His mind stuttered when he realized Jamie could have easily come up here when he'd gotten no answer on Meg's phone.

Or Tuck might have decided to pop in. The clothes in the living room would have been impossible to explain. Thank God their cleaning lady, who was a terrible gossip, only showed up once a week. She'd been there the day before getting the place spotless for Meg's visit.

On his way back down the hall to throw their stuff in each of their respective bedrooms, he nearly ran over Meg barging out of the bathroom. He screeched to a halt.

"I thought you'd left," she said as she pulled a blue knit top over her head.

He followed her into her bedroom and dumped her clothes on the bed. "I decided to do some damage control first."

She glanced at her clothes in horror. "Omigod. Is there any other evidence?"

"Not really. The kitchen's a mess, and our dishes are still on the coffee table, but that doesn't indicate that we—"

"Good." She quickly stepped into the black pants he'd ironed. "And thanks, again. We absolutely can't let anyone know." She buttoned and zipped with amazing speed.

"They won't hear it from me."

"Or me." She yanked the black fringed jacket from its hanger at the same time she shoved her feet into a pair of black slides. "I see you're wearing jeans."

He gazed at her. "I figure I can trust you not to throw me in front of the camera."

"Of course I won't do that." She buttoned the jacket and grabbed her laptop. "That's it. I'm ready. Which way to the bunkhouse?"

He hadn't thought about her not knowing her way around. "What were you planning to do if I'd already left?"

"Go outside and circle the house, looking for the white van. But that would take extra time. I also could have called Jamie on the cell and asked for directions."

He should have known she'd have backup plans. A woman didn't get where she was without being resourceful. "Let me get rid of these clothes and I'll take you there."

"Hurry. Every second counts."

"I'll hurry." He lengthened his stride as he headed down the hall. In the bedroom he didn't waste time looking at the bed where they'd had the orgasm fest she'd asked for. He just threw down his clothes, snatched up his hat and clapped it on his head.

He found her pacing the living room. "Back door's closest." He led the way through the dining room and was nearly into the kitchen when he realized she wasn't right behind him.

Instead she stood in the living room, staring at him in a dazed sort of way.

"Get a move on, Meg! I thought you were in a hurry."

She blinked and walked quickly forward. "I am. Let's go."

"Is something wrong?" He opened the back door and gestured her out ahead of him.

"No, no. I mean, other than the obvious, that I'm horribly late."

He decided not to press her on it. The morning was brisk, and he took a deep breath of cool air, which steadied him. "This way." He started down an incline toward the bunkhouse about fifty yards away.

The van's antenna was cranked up, and the thing was huge, out of proportion with the van. With all the equipment, it looked as if alien spacecraft had landed, but he remembered from watching a movie being made in Sonoita that the big canvas things on tripods were actually lights. Electrical cords ran inside to the bunkhouse.

Jamie, headphones plastered to his ears, hurried in and out of the van. Jed and Denny milled around as if trying to help. Most likely they were getting in Jamie's way.

Tuck stood over by the barn with a small crowd of maybe ten people. Clint recognized cowhands from the area, a couple of wives and one girlfriend. No doubt they were all here to get a glimpse of Meg.

For the first time Clint understood that his time alone with her the previous night had been a rare occurrence. He'd had her all to himself because she hadn't yet made her first appearance in the community. No one had dared to come up to the house and ask to see her, but now that she was broadcasting the morning show, they felt comfortable showing up.

He wished he could somehow skip back to the beginning of their short relationship and go through it again. Only this time he'd savor everything more, because he'd have a deeper appreciation for the special treat he'd been given. He'd had no right to be grumpy this morning when she'd launched into her star routine. She was, after all, famous.

"Are you doing okay?" he asked, glancing sideways at her.

"Fine. Just keep going."

"This isn't the best footing for your shoes." How she navigated in those backless wonders he'd never know, but she didn't seem the least impaired as she hurried along beside him. He didn't offer to take her arm, not wanting to be seen touching her at all.

"I can manage. Listen, when we get there, I need to get organized for the broadcast, so I won't have time to deal with that group of people."

"I'll make sure they don't bother you."

"Don't be hard on them. Just let them know I have limited time to get on the satellite."

"I'll explain it."

"Tell me your foreman's name again. I know I should remember, but my brain is mush right now. Tanner? Turner?"

"Tucker. He asked you to call him Tuck, though." Clint wished he'd brought his shades. Without them he'd have to be very careful of his expression when he glanced her way. Tuck had known him for a long time, had even been around during a couple of his lovesick phases, and Tuck would catch on fast if Clint cast even one longing glance in Meg's direction.

"That's right. Tucker Benson. Tuck." She took a shaky breath. "I wish you'd reconsider and go on camera. You're exactly what people think of when they picture a cowboy."

"Sorry, no can do."

"All right. Then here we go." She smiled and waved at he crowd. "Catch you all after the broadcast, okay?" she called out. "Tuck, I need you over here by the van."

"Yes, ma'am." Tuck, dressed in his newest shirt and sporting his favorite silver belt buckle, walked toward amie.

"I already have him miked," Jamie said out as they neared the van. "Go get your mike. Got a script?"

Meg tapped the case of her laptop. "Wrote it yesterday."

"Need cues?"

"Nope, I'll remember it." She glanced at Clint. "If you won't go on camera, will you at least let me borrow your hat?"

Instinctively he grabbed the brim of his cherished Stetson in a possessive hold. It had been a present from his dad a year before he'd died. Nobody wore Clint's hat besides Clint. "Uh, what for?"

"I'm having an incredibly bad hair day, and the hat will help. It'll look as if I've gone native if I wear it. Don't worry—I won't mention where I got it."

Because she was a New Yorker, she wouldn't understand how he felt about this hat. After all the intimacies they'd shared, withholding his hat would seem unreasonable to her. He took it off and handed it over.

"Thanks." She grasped the crown and settled the hat on her head with the brim tipped back, so it wouldn't put her ace in shadow. "How's that?"

He gulped and nodded. "Fine. Just fine." But she looked more than fine. Damned if she didn't look perfect in the hat, as if she'd been made to wear it. Of course a real cowgirl would pull it forward so that it blocked the sun the

way it was supposed to, but Meg was still a natural for tha
old Stetson.

He had the ridiculous idea to give it to her as a souve
nir. How stupid was that? Once home, she'd probably
throw it in the corner of her closet.

"Meg, three minutes!" Jamie called.

"I'm on it!" Then she glanced at Clint. "Go over there
and placate those people, okay?"

"Right." The onlookers were staying right next to the
corral and making no move to interfere, but Meg seemed
determined to give him a job that took him away from the
van. He had the oddest feeling that if he stayed, he'd make
her nervous.

In a small way, that comforted him. He didn't want to
be the reason she loused up the broadcast, but he didn'
want to think that she could easily dismiss what had hap
pened, either. By sending him away, she'd shown that she
was vulnerable. He'd hold onto that thought as a consola
tion prize.

MEG HAD DONE live feeds before, but from the streets o
New York instead of the fields of Arizona. Earlier this yea
"Meg and Mel in the Morning" had run a segment in
which she'd asked pedestrians a different question every
morning. But she'd been on familiar ground then. And a
man she'd been having sex with the night before hadn'
been standing only a few yards away.

Jamie balanced the camera on his shoulder. "I want you
and Tuck over there, with that weathered gray wall behind
you," he said.

"Got it." Grabbing her lapel mike and battery pack, she
motioned Tuck to stand beside her. But as she attached her
battery pack to her waistband at the small of her back, she

remembered the sweet pressure of Clint's hand there. As she ran her mike up under the front of her jacket and clipped it on, she remembered how his gentle caress had become urgent, his kisses deeper…

"Meg, don't space out on me," Jamie said. "Didn't get much sleep, huh, kid?"

"Uh, not a lot. Too quiet out here in the boonies." She managed a smile as she tucked her earpiece in place.

"Thirty-second commercial break," Jamie said. "Let's check everything out. Mel and Mona, how are we looking?" He glanced at Meg. "Mona wants to know if the hat is because of a bad hair day."

Meg stood up straighter and worked not to clench her jaw, which would make her look grim instead of perky. "Who has time to worry about hair? I'm too busy looking at cute buns in tight denim to give a damn." Whoops. She'd meant to say "give a hoot" instead of "give a damn." Her nerves were a wee bit on edge.

"Mona also wants to know why your chin is pink," Jamie said as he focused the camera.

Mona can bite my… "Sunburn," Meg said with another smile.

"And Mel wants to know why you're not on a horse."

Somehow Meg kept her smile in place. She'd never been on a horse in her life. After the incident at the parade, she'd avoided horses completely. "No time for that," she said.

"Tip the hat up a bit more," Jamie said.

Meg adjusted the hat.

Jamie held up his hand, fingers raised. "Five seconds."

As Jamie silently counted down the seconds, Meg cleared her throat and moistened her lips. Then Jamie pointed to her, and she was live, coast-to-coast, beaming into the living rooms, kitchens and family rooms of America. She never failed to get a charge out of that.

The time went like lightning. She worked in her reference to the Mustang Mountains and the historic nature of the ranch, hoping George would see this segment and give Clint a break.

After that brief introduction, she interviewed Tuck about his day-to-day routine, and his shyness in front of the camera made him seem like the strong, silent type. Then Meg promised viewers that she'd have three hot cowboy finalists on the air the following morning.

Jamie gave her the signal, and the broadcast was over.

"Good job," Jamie called over to her as he lifted the camera from his shoulder. "You ever been on a horse?"

"Nope." She started taking off her equipment. "Why?" She had a bad feeling about that question.

"Mel wants everyone on horseback tomorrow. You and the three finalists."

Meg groaned. "I'll bet that was Mona's idea." Maybe somehow Mona had found out she was afraid of horses.

"We can find you a real tame one," Tuck said. "Don't worry about it."

"I'll need the oldest and slowest nag on the place," she said. "If you have one named Dobbin, that would be my horse. By the way, you were great on the air. Thank you." She decided not to think about the horse thing. That was tomorrow.

"No problem." He appeared pleased with himself now that it was over. "Anytime you need me, just holler."

"Thanks, I will." She felt restless and disoriented now that the broadcast was finished. Compared to the hour she was used to spending in the limelight, this seemed minuscule. She was like a runner who'd been taken out of the race a few yards out of the starting block. She wanted more air time.

But she wouldn't be getting that until this gig was over, and if Mona stole her spot, she might never have that kind of air time again. She hoped she hadn't looked as disheveled on camera as she'd felt. Maybe the hat had been too cutesie, but considering how her hair had looked this morning, it had been a dire necessity.

Besides, wearing it had felt good, a kind of talisman to see her through. She'd needed the hat nearby, but not the guy who owned it. Even now she started to shake when she realized he'd watched the whole performance. Strange, when nobody else made her nervous. But nobody else had ever gotten so close, so fast.

And now she had to act as if they were nothing but casual friends. She walked toward the group of people standing beside the barn. "I want to thank all of you for being so quiet during the broadcast," she said. "Now if I can answer any questions, or—"

"Can we get an autograph?" called out a brunette in jeans and a denim jacket.

"Of course."

And just like that, Meg was surrounded by people holding pictures of her, magazine articles about her and even a *TV Guide* opened to the page where "Meg and Mel in the Morning" was listed.

She signed autographs and talked to a crowd that seemed to grow bigger by the moment. Jed and Denny, Clint's other two employees, finally made their way over and asked for an autograph.

Jed looked like a linebacker in cowboy clothes, and redheaded Denny had enough freckles to brand him forever as the cute and wholesome type. Of the two, she thought

Denny had a better chance of making the finals, if he loosened up a little. But she could tell from the way they both stumbled over their words that they were scared to death of her. No wonder they'd stayed in the bunkhouse the night before.

So her star power had given her one night of privacy, one night to be alone with Clint. From the eagerness of the people surrounding her now, she doubted that she'd have any more privacy while she was in Sonoita. Today she'd be mingling with everyone at the rodeo grounds as cowboys came to compete in the contest. By the end of the day she'd be an adopted member of the community, and if she valued her ratings she wouldn't go into hiding tonight.

At one point she glanced up from the *People* magazine cover she was signing and searched the crowd for Clint. He'd moved a distance away and stood watching her. She caught his eye for one tiny moment, and in that split second she knew that he understood. They'd grabbed their one shining opportunity to be alone, and now it was gone.

10

CLINT COULD FIND no good excuse to hang out with Meg as she moved through her scheduled activities. Plenty of people were ready to do anything she asked, from bringing her coffee to loaning her a pair of sunglasses. By ten in the morning the crowd had started for the rodeo grounds where the contestants would show off their roping and riding skills.

"You going along?" Tuck asked as the van carrying Jamie and Meg pulled out, followed by a procession of pickup trucks.

"I…" Clint couldn't decide. Nobody would miss him if he stayed behind and he hated the idea of being lumped in with the rest of her attentive fans. He was more than that, dammit. But maybe not anymore.

"Aw, come on." Tuck said. "This doesn't happen every day. I'll drive my truck. You can ride with me."

"Can I borrow a hat?" Clint felt naked without his, especially if they were going to spend the rest of the morning at the rodeo grounds, where all the cowboys would have on hats. Luckily he and Tuck wore the same size.

"You sure can. Let me duck into the bunkhouse and fetch you one." In no time Tuck was back with his old summer straw. "It's not right for the weather, but it'll keep the sun out of your eyes."

"It'll work. Thanks." Clint put on the hat and walked with Tuck over to a dusty pickup parked beside the bunkhouse.

"What happened to your city slicker routine?"

Clint shrugged. "She's smarter than I thought. She saw right through me, so I had to confess."

"That didn't take long." Tuck smiled. "You gonna enter her contest?"

"Not on your life." Clint got into the truck and slammed the door with more force than was necessary.

Tuck climbed in the driver's side and coaxed the ancient engine to life. Then he glanced sideways at Clint as he let out the clutch and started down the rutted road. "You two get along okay last night?"

"Yeah, we managed." Clint gripped the dash as the truck bounced along.

"Eating in front of the fire worked out?"

Clint stared straight ahead through the bug-spattered windshield and wished he'd ridden with someone else. He hadn't counted on Tuck giving him the third degree. "Yeah. She liked José's enchiladas."

"Don't take this the wrong way, but ever since you two walked out of the house this morning, you've behaved like a man with a cattle prod up his ass."

That was probably true, and he didn't want Meg to catch him acting that way. He'd have to lighten up. "You know I've never liked the idea of this whole deal, Tuck. I'm merely tolerating it because I have no choice."

"I thought it was good, what she said about the history of the Circle W. George might think twice about turning it into a subdivision and golf course once he hears that."

Clint nodded. He'd appreciated that part of the broadcast. "Maybe. But don't count on it."

"Wouldn't dream of it, Mr. Sunshine. I would hate for

a ray of hope to sneak in and spoil that sour mood of yours."

Clint said nothing. He couldn't very well deny he was in a sour mood. He'd work on it before he saw Meg again.

"She's pretty."

The comment had been made so quietly that Clint had to glance over and see if Tuck had actually spoken. "You say something?"

"I said she's real pretty. Can't believe that point is entirely lost on you."

"I suppose not." Clint returned his attention to the view out the windshield. *Pretty* didn't even begin to cover how he saw Meg. She was the most beautiful woman he'd ever known, and that was both with or without her clothes. He might have been better off without that knowledge, but he didn't regret one second of the time he'd had with her.

"You two looked mighty fine together when you came walking down the hill to the bunkhouse this morning."

"So what?"

"Nothing." Tuck found a parking spot in the dirt lot in back of the grandstand. "Just making an observation."

Clint found it ludicrous that Tuck seemed to be in a matchmaking frame of mind, but that was how he was coming across. That whole business with the cushion placement the night before might have been part of some harebrained attempt to create a romance.

But they'd had sex, not romance, and that was all they'd ever have. Tuck needed to back off. Clint turned to him. "Let me make an observation, then. Meg and I have absolutely nothing in common. She's a big-time TV celebrity and I'm just…a cowboy. So whatever crazy things are going through your mind, forget it."

Tuck held up both hands. "I'm not thinking anything!"

"Good. Thanks for the ride." Taking a deep breath, Clint got out of the truck. No matter how much effort it took, he would be cheerful for the rest of the day. Anyone he met from now on would be greeted with a shit-eating grin, even if it killed him.

Four hours later, he'd concluded that it just might. He had grinned so damned much his jaw ached. They'd finished at the rodeo grounds and most of the people had come back to the Circle W for a picnic lunch José had thrown together. Then Meg had set up in the living room so that she could do individual interviews with the cowboys. They each had fifteen minutes with her.

Clint had helped José clean up after lunch, and he was constantly aware of Meg in there talking quietly with the contestants. He told himself that being jealous served no purpose whatsoever, but those interviews were too damned cozy to suit him.

The living room belonged to him and Meg. It was their special place, and nobody else should be in there alone with her. Then he had a horrible thought—that Meg might have propositioned any guy she'd been stuck with last night, considering that she'd finally had a chance to escape her role of wholesome TV personality for a few hours. No, he couldn't believe that. They'd shared something special.

Yet that something special seemed to be slipping away with every minute that passed. When he overheard Meg telling Denny she was looking for that "killer cowboy charm," he decided to head for the hills. On top of battling jealousy, he'd rather not listen while Meg commercialized everything he held dear. He needed to take his gelding Nugget for a long ride instead of hanging around the ranch house.

The weather had turned cooler, so he went back to his bedroom, once again ignoring the rumpled bed, and took his denim jacket out of the closet. Adjusting the lamb's-wool collar, he walked through the living room on his way out the back door. He hadn't intended to speak to Meg, because she seemed involved in her interview with Denny.

But as he was leaving, she called after him. "Um, Clint, you look as if you're taking off somewhere."

He turned back. "Thought I'd go for a ride and check the fence." It was a lame excuse, which Denny would realize but she wouldn't. Now that they weren't running cattle, the condition of the fence wasn't nearly as important. He still checked it out of habit, but not often, and he'd been around the perimeter just last month.

"Oh." She cleared her throat. "Well, I don't want to interfere with the running of the ranch."

"Is there something you need?" How dumb that they were standing there talking to each other like polite acquaintances when the night before they'd been moaning in the grip of mutual pleasure.

"You probably remember that I'll be announcing the finalists tonight."

"I know." And after the broadcast tomorrow morning, she'd be leaving. He was trying not to think about that.

"We're going to have a pre-announcement party at the bar in the Steak Out. I wondered…if you'd be going."

He couldn't tell from her expression if she wanted him to or not. One thing was certain—they wouldn't be repeating their intimate dinner of the previous night.

"If you have other things to do, I understand," she said, eyeing him with those big brown eyes. "I just thought, if you weren't busy, that—"

"Of course I'll be there." And he'd drink soda. Alcohol

wasn't a wise idea when he had to watch everything he said and did.

"Thanks." She sent him her megawatt smile.

His heart pounded faster, just from the electricity of that smile. He looked away before Denny had a chance to see something more than polite interest in his eyes.

"We've planned to start around six," Meg said.

"I'll be back before then. Have fun." He left quickly, eager to saddle up and ride off his frustration. Tonight would take all his resources, and he needed some solitude to fortify himself.

MEG DIDN'T DARE allow herself the luxury of watching Clint walk away. Instead she flipped on the tape recorder and turned to Denny. "So you've competed in how many rodeos?"

Although Denny had seemed intimidated by her at first, she'd worked him through that, and now he was Gabby Gus. He described his bull-riding experiences in great detail, and because the tape recorder caught it all, Meg could daydream about Clint.

He was killing her. He'd started the process this morning when he'd nearly collided with her in the hall. Once she'd seen him in boots, jeans and a chambray Western shirt, she'd worked hard not to drool.

Then he'd added the hat, and the effect of seeing him as a full-fledged cowboy had stopped her in her tracks. With time at a premium and Jamie waiting impatiently down by the van, she'd ignored everything except the picture Clint made decked out in his cowboy gear.

She'd borrowed his hat to hide her bad hair, but she'd also snagged the hat in self-defense. She was ready to do nearly anything to lessen the impact of his cowboyness and save her sanity. Then he'd found another hat, and now he'd added a denim jacket with a lamb's-wool collar. And he was going out to ride his horse. She was ready to attack him.

Instead she'd casually asked him to have drinks with her and a cast of thousands. At least it would seem like thousands when all she wanted was another night alone with her fantasy cowboy. No denying it—if she put in a special order for the man of her dreams, he would look exactly like Clint.

What a shame that he'd turned up his nose at her contest. Tuck had been great to have on the morning's segment, but interviewing Clint would have taken ratings through the roof. Then, if he were a contestant, he'd generate even more interest in the contest. She felt it in her gut, knew it would be good for the show.

And she thought it would be good for Clint, too. Even though she'd seen only the Arizona candidates so far, she didn't have to travel to the other states to know that Clint would have an excellent chance of winning. He had it all—rugged good looks, ranching skills and sexual charisma.

If he would only enter the contest, magical things could happen. Reality TV had shown how the public embraced the finalists in a contest like this. Even if Clint didn't win, simply being on television would bring offers for commercials, appearances, maybe even a movie role.

She would be there to guide him through unfamiliar territory, and they might even figure out a way to continue their relationship. But even more important, he might earn enough to buy back his beloved ranch.

"So do you think I have a chance?" Denny asked after he'd run out of bull-riding stories.

"Absolutely." She switched off the tape recorder. Denny

was adorable. A rakish grin along with his All-American freckles and red hair would make him a fan favorite, although personally Meg thought he wasn't quite sexy enough to take the title of Hottest Cowboy in the West. He might be a finalist, though, whereas Jed probably wouldn't make it. Jed threw a mean rope in the arena, but he'd indulged in too many beers and had the belly to show it.

Cowboys had arrived from all over Arizona, and if she could, she'd pack up every last one and give them a shot at fame and fortune. She hadn't planned on letting her emotions get involved in the contest. Here she was at the beginning of the competition and already she didn't want to disappoint anyone. Tonight she'd have to pick three finalists, and that would be much tougher than she'd imagined.

"I'm glad you thought up this contest," Denny said. "When Mel said on TV that there weren't any more real cowboys, me and the guys wanted to head to New York and prove him wrong. But right away you set this contest up, which will show him we really do exist."

"The contest wouldn't have worked if all of you hadn't turned out. I appreciate that. I realize that some people think the idea's…silly." And if everyone had taken Clint's attitude, she would have been dead in the water.

"You mean the boss. He's a private kind of guy, sort of a throw-back to the old days. Asking him to compete for a spot on a television program would be like expecting a wild stallion to wear ribbons and prance around a show ring."

"I suppose." But she'd love to find a way to get him into the contest, and she was running out of time. Being part of the process might give him his ranch…and her. Twenty-four hours ago she'd thought marriage was a distant dream, one to be postponed until she'd solidified her position as a celebrity. Her thinking was changing in light of what she'd found with Clint. She hoped he felt the same.

The front door opened and Bill, a contestant from Prescott, walked in. "Okay, Denny, get on outta here and let a real man have some time with the lady."

"Who?" Denny stood and glanced around. "What real man? All I see is a broken-down, bandy-legged cowpoke making way too much noise."

Bill grinned. "Yeah, and all I see is a sad-looking saddle tramp who'll be mucking out stalls while yours truly is taking a bite out of the Big Apple. Isn't that right, Meg?"

"My lips are sealed until tonight." But she thought both Bill and Denny would end up making the top three. Bill had a little too much swagger to suit her, but his blond good looks would play well on camera, and he did great things for a pair of jeans.

"Come on over and sit down, Bill," she said. "And tell me all about yourself. And thanks, Denny."

"My pleasure." Denny left, giving Bill a good-natured punch on the arm on his way out.

Meg settled in for her next interview. But all through it, and the six that followed, she thought about Clint, the perfect candidate. She had to talk him into it.

Then, after the last contestant had left, and she was headed to her bathroom to take a shower, inspiration hit. She ran for her cell phone and dialed Sharon, catching her out having a drink with some girlfriends.

"I'm sorry to bother you." Meg had to raise her voice so that her executive producer could hear inside the noisy bar. "But I need permission to add something to the contest."

"Like what?"

"In case I come across a situation when I can't narrow the field to three, I want permission to add a fourth. I'll only do it once, and he'll be called Meg's Pick. Can I do that?"

"Sure, why not?" Sharon sounded in a good mood, as if the ratings news had been good.

"Thanks. Talk to you later!" Meg hung up feeling as if she'd saved the day. Clint wouldn't have to compete, wouldn't have to be a stallion forced into parading around a ring with ribbons in his mane. He could simply become Meg's Pick. How much easier could it be than that?

CLINT WALKED BACK into the house at five. The living room was empty, and the only noise came from the shower in the second bathroom. He didn't have to think very hard about who was in there.

He'd known they would likely end up alone in the house again, probably tonight after the shindig at the Steak Out. After three hours of riding across the foothills of the Mustang Mountains, he still didn't know the best way to handle whatever time he had left with Meg. Part of the answer was up to her, of course, but if she asked for more of what they'd had the night before, could he handle that?

He wanted her desperately, and that scared him. One more night in her arms would probably make him feel worse when she left. And they continued to run the risk that someone would find out.

But as he stood listening to the shower run, knowing she was in there naked, he realized he wasn't strong enough to turn her down. If she wanted to crawl into his bed again tonight, he'd welcome her there and deal with the consequences later.

For now, he'd head for his own shower. With only an

hour before they had to be at the Steak Out, he'd be a fool to go into that guest bathroom. But how he wanted to. How he wished that he could shuck his clothes, step into that tub with her and do what he'd been thinking about all day.

Instead he walked into his bedroom, peeling off clothes as he went. Damn, he was hard already from the knowledge that the only thing separating his naked body from hers was willpower. He was running low on willpower.

But he forced himself to climb into his shower. The shower head still dangled free, and he reattached it to the bracket before turning on the water. The pulsing jets came on, and he twisted the outer ring until he had a fine spray again.

Tough guys with an erection were supposed to take cold showers. At least that's what he'd heard. He hated cold showers, so he reached for the soap and tried to ignore his very stiff buddy.

Instead of the soap, he touched the condom packet he'd laid there the night before and never used. With a snort of frustration, he threw the packet out onto the bath mat. Now he was harder still.

Hell, this was no way to take a shower, with one very sensitive part of him sticking out like a riding crop. He had an option, but he hesitated to take it. He hadn't locked his bedroom door, and he couldn't be positive that she'd have sense enough to stay in her part of the house until they were safely on their way to the Steak Out.

However, with the pressure he felt down below he could finish himself off in no time. And if he didn't do something to remedy the situation, he wouldn't be able to get his jeans buttoned. He gave up and took a firm grip on the problem.

"Clint?"

His hand stilled. She sounded as if she might be standing right outside the shower. "Uh, yeah?" Life didn't get much crazier than this.

"I came out of the bathroom and heard your shower going."

He took a breath and tried to forget about orgasms. "I needed to get cleaned up for tonight."

"Me, too. But I...had an idea."

"What's that?"

"I can't speak for you, but I'm feeling a little bit on edge."

You want to talk about feeling on edge? Try teetering on the brink of a climax while trying to carry on a normal conversation.

"So I wondered if you might be in the same fix."

He swallowed. "I'm not sure what you mean."

"Well, I found this." The condom packet came sailing back into the shower and landed at his feet. He turned to find her standing at the entrance to the shower, her hair slicked back from her face and not a stitch on.

Her glance moved downward and she smiled. "It's nice to know I'm in good company." Then she joined him in the shower.

11

ALTHOUGH THEY HAD no time to waste, Meg cautioned herself to let Clint make the next move. His body was doing plenty of talking, but he hadn't said a thing out loud. If he told her this was a bad idea, she'd accept that and leave the shower.

She hoped he wouldn't. Being in this shower aroused her like an intimate caress, and she trembled with longing. The familiar scent of soap and desire stirred memories of a fabulous orgasm. The rush of water had become a sexual signal, as had the smooth tiles beneath her bare feet and the riot of colorful flowers painted on the clay.

He held her gaze. "We can't forget the time. People will get suspicious."

"I won't forget the time." She mentally crossed her fingers. "This won't take long…for either of us."

He was breathing hard, staring at her with heat in his eyes. "So you want efficiency."

"Something like that."

"All right." He broke eye contact long enough to reach for the condom packet at his feet. Then he pinned her with his gaze, not bothering to look at what he was doing as he tore open the packet and rolled on the condom. Now that was talent.

Then he grasped her hips, his grip firm with purpose

as he backed her up against the wall. "Put your hands on my shoulders."

Looking deep into his eyes, she rested her hands on his shoulders as if they were about to execute a complicated Latin dance step. His skin was wet and warm. She loved feeling his muscles move as he tightened his hold on her hips.

"When I lift you, put your legs around my waist."

She nodded, her heart beating furiously, her body aching and quivering with anticipation. Then he picked her up, and in one fluid motion she wrapped her legs around him. At nearly the same moment he slid smoothly inside her.

Oh, yes. She vibrated with pleasure, and a soft hum of delight rose from her throat.

His pupils dilated until his eyes were more black than blue, and his voice shook with emotion. "I've thought about this all day." He adjusted his stance, which allowed him to probe even deeper.

"Me…too. Oh, that's good."

"Meg, you turn me inside out."

"Sorry."

"Not your fault. Now hang on."

She tightened her grip on his shoulders. "I'm ready."

"Yeah, you are. I've never felt so welcomed." His fingers flexed against her bottom as he began to thrust, slowly at first, then faster.

Propped against the hard tile, she became pliable dough he kneaded and shaped into the perfect receptacle for the rhythmic motion of his penis. Her body responded to each stroke with another layer of delicious pressure. Soon. Very soon.

His breath came in ragged gasps. "Close?"

"Yes." She began to pant. "Oh, yes…now…now!" She bucked in his arms as a climax overtook her.

With a groan he pushed home and closed his eyes. Then he held on tight as his body shook and he gulped for air.

At last his body stilled and he opened his eyes. "Incredible," he murmured.

"I know."

"I can't believe you're leaving tomorrow."

She struggled for breath so she could speak. "About that…we need to talk."

He leaned forward and kissed her gently. "No, we don't. I didn't mean that to sound like I expected more."

"That's not what I meant. I—"

"Let's get dressed." He kissed her lightly again. "We don't want to be late."

Maybe she should postpone what she had to say. It wasn't a discussion she wanted to rush through. "Okay, we'll get dressed. We can talk later on tonight."

He smiled. "Sure you want to waste time talking?"

She started to tell him it wouldn't be a waste, that their discussion could change their lives. But now wasn't the time. "I promise not to waste a single minute of being alone with you," she said.

"That's all I ask."

BY SOME MIRACLE Clint and Meg left the house and climbed into his pickup truck at ten minutes before six. She'd insisted on returning his hat, so he wore it and she went bareheaded. The hat smelled of her hair spray, and ordinarily he'd be ticked off about that, but she had the power to do just about anything and get away with it.

But now that they were in the truck and on their way, he was worried that she'd use this time to get into her "discussion." He had a good idea how that would go. First she'd tell him how much this time together had meant to her. He believed it had meant quite a bit, so that was fine.

She wouldn't be able to leave it at that, though. Eventually she'd begin to apologize because she couldn't keep seeing him, and to hear her laying out all the reasons would depress the hell out of him. Intellectually he understood the problems. If his heart didn't get any of it, too bad. He'd deal. She didn't have to rub his nose in it, though.

"This is perfect," she said as they started down the dirt road to the highway. "My stay wouldn't be complete without a ride in a pickup."

"This isn't just any pickup, either," he said, switching on the headlights. "Allow me to introduce Esmerelda."

"Really?" She laughed. "I'm glad to meet you, Esmerelda. I'm dying to know how you got your name. One of Clint's old girlfriends?"

"I wish I'd had a girlfriend as reliable as Esmerelda. It's a Greek name that means emerald. This truck's green and she's a gem."

"That's wonderful. I love it." She hesitated. "I don't suppose…"

He could predict what was coming.

"I don't suppose you'd let me use that in tomorrow's broadcast?"

Yep, just what he'd expected. He glanced at her. "I don't suppose I would. Low profile, remember?"

She sighed. "I remember. But I don't see how talking about your truck would be such a big problem. I don't have to say it's *your* truck."

"Everyone around here would know, anyway."

"So why not let me talk about it? I don't understand why it would bother you."

In some ways he was closer to her than to any woman he'd known. In other ways they were oceans apart. "That's because you're used to having lots of people know what's going on in your life. I'm not. To me it would feel like an invasion of privacy." He changed the subject, determined to steer the conversation away from any unwelcome topics. "Have you decided on the three finalists?"

"Yes, and I don't know if I can stand seeing the faces of the guys who aren't chosen. Between now and the time I end this trip in Wyoming, I need to toughen up."

Although he was touched that she cared that much, he thought her concern was unnecessary. "You don't have to worry about cowboys, Meg. They've competed in roping and riding events ever since they were kids. They can handle rejection." *And so can I, so don't think you have to mollycoddle me.*

"I'm sure they can, but this might be different than going for a trophy or a cash prize. Besides the cash award, this is a chance to be on national TV."

"Trust me, although they'd be thrilled to make it, TV isn't their life the way it is yours. They won't react like you would if you lost a chance like this."

"You don't think any of them want a shot at doing something else?"

Clint waited for one lone vehicle to pass before turning onto the paved two-lane highway. "Nope. They just want something to brag about to their grandkids." He gestured toward the darkening landscape, where rolling hills gave way to the jagged silhouette of the Santa Ritas on the far side of the valley. Pinpricks of light were just beginning to flicker in the navy sky. "See that?"

"See what? It's all dark out there."

"Exactly. Only a few lights from ranch houses scattered

here and there, which means lots of open space, the exact opposite of a big city. We all live here because we crave room to roam around."

"But don't you get bored? There's not even a movie theater."

"I guess it's all in what you get used to. You're used to living at top speed, keeping yourself entertained all the time. Out here things go a lot slower. We watch sunsets. We take long horseback rides. We sit around the fire and talk. Or not talk. There's a whole lot of silence out here in the country, and that's how we like it."

But even as he described his idyllic picture of Sonoita, he admitted it was more of a sentimental memory than a promise of what was ahead for this area. The sprinkling of lights on the landscape had become more dense just in the past year. Not so long ago none of the streets had been named, but now they all had some kind of designation so they could have 911 emergency response.

"I have to admit I haven't missed the sirens," she said.

"But you've missed the excitement of the city?"

She laughed. "No, not with you around. You're Bloomie's, Saks and *Late Show with David Letterman* all rolled into one."

He put on his turn signal and pulled into the parking lot of the Steak Out. The place was packed, which didn't surprise him. "That's probably because I'm new and exotic. Another few days with me and you'd discover all my bad habits."

"Like what?" She made no move to unlatch her seat belt and get out.

He shut off the motor and turned to her. "Oh, the usual. I squeeze the toothpaste in the middle and leave the coffee grounds in the pot for hours. I sing off-key and hog the overs and cut articles out of the Sunday paper before nybody else has read it. Stuff like that."

"Sounds kind of nice."

"Then you must have lived with some real losers. The lirty-underwear-on-the-floor and greasy-dishes-in-the-ink category of guys."

"I've never lived with a guy," she said softly.

"Never? I thought that was what everyone did in the ig city. I know what you said about your recent situation, ut before that—"

"Before that I was so busy climbing up the ladder I lidn't have the time or patience for a full-time relation-hip." In the pale light filtering into the cab from the res-aurant windows, her expression grew wistful. "I've told nyself I didn't need that, at least not until I've secured my pot."

"And you're probably right. Sex is one thing, but you lon't need somebody hanging around all the time, man-;ling your toothpaste tube."

"You know what one of my favorite parts of this trip has een so far?"

The conversation was getting dangerously intimate, ut he didn't know how to sidetrack it without sounding s nervous as he felt. "Let me guess. Something to do with ny latest home improvement project, aka the shower." Ie didn't think she meant anything sexual, but he would ry and make a joke, anyway.

"You have an awesome shower, and I've loved every ninute of getting naked with you, but do you remember vhen I first arrived, and we sat out on the porch?"

"Yeah, I remember." He remembered every waking sec-nd with her.

"Nobody sits on porches where I live, obviously. If anyone had told me it was fun to sit on the porch and stare out at a whole lot of nothing, I would have laughed. But keep coming back to that porch thing. While we sat there talking, I felt…relaxed. I'm thinking it might have something to do with staring at nothing."

"Could be." His chest felt tight. She was beginning to fall in love with the wide-open spaces, but she wouldn't have the time or luxury to complete the process. They would never know if she might eventually get hooked on staring at nothing. But knowing that she might, if given a chance, filled him with regret. "Listen, we should go in. I'm sure everyone is impatiently waiting for the honored guest."

She reached over and squeezed his hand. "Let's have signal for when one of us is ready to leave."

"Okay." He would be ready five minutes after the walked in the door.

"How about scratching our noses? If either of u scratches our nose, that means we want to go. But if it' bad timing for the other one, the opposite signal is running your tongue over your lower lip."

"That's no good."

"Why not?"

"If you run your tongue over your lower lip, I'm going to want to rip your clothes off."

"Oh." She laughed. "Okay, then how about eyebrow lifting? Will that get you hot?"

"Watching you walk across the room gets me hot."

"Yeah?" She sounded delighted with the news.

"Yeah. But we can go with eyebrow lifting. Come or The sooner we get in there, the sooner we can leave."

THE BAR WAS JAMMED and noisy, but once Meg walked in everyone stopped talking and stared at her. The onl sound came from the two televisions mounted above the bar, where a Suns basketball game was in progress.

For one scary moment Meg was afraid they knew what she and Clint had been up to an hour ago. "Is there a problem?" she asked, praying there wasn't.

"No problem," said the bartender. "I think we're a little star-struck, is all. What'll you have? It's on the house."

"No, I'm buying," called a cowboy from the back.

"No, you aren't," said another one, slapping his money on the bar. Then mayhem broke out as nearly every man in the place jockeyed for a spot at the bar, each waving money and insisting they were buying Meg Delancy a drink.

Jamie pushed through the crowd and came over to her. "Man, oh, man, this'll take all freakin' day. I know. I'll jus' make you somethin'. Whatcha want? You, too, pardner." He slapped Clint on the back and giggled. "Pardner. I'm really gettin' into this."

Meg peered at her cameraman. "Jamie, are you drunk?"

Jamie gave her a silly grin. "Doin' my best to be. Still too sober, though. Too damned sober."

Meg linked her arm through Jamie's. "Come with me for a minute." She glanced up at Clint. "Excuse us—we'll be right back."

With the hubbub still going on about who would buy drinks, nobody seemed to notice as she guided Jamie through the doorway into the reception area of the restaurant that was adjacent to the bar. Not a soul was in the restaurant. Everyone in town was obviously crammed into the saloon.

Meg led Jamie over to a row of chairs intended for people waiting for a table. From the way he was weaving, she thought he'd be better off sitting than standing. She gave him a gentle nudge in that direction and he sank down onto the nearest chair.

"Okay." She took the chair next to him. "This is so not like you. What's happened?"

His expression grew mournful. "Called my darling Alison this afternoon."

Meg closed her eyes, afraid of what he was about to say.

"Found herself another guy. I've been gone less 'n two days." He held up three fingers, studied them and pulled one finger down. "Two days."

"Jamie, I'm so sorry. That sucks."

"Two days! How could somethin' happen in two lousy days?"

She was the wrong person to ask a question like that. Two days had made a huge difference in her life. When she'd left New York she'd imagined herself staying single for years. Now she was trying to figure out a way to be with Clint. She was thinking long-term, maybe very long-term. Like forever.

"I wanna go home," Jamie said. "Get a look at him. Try 'n get her back."

At first she panicked. Losing Jamie could jeopardize the whole trip. Nobody else had his eye for composition. Any other cameraman they sent had the potential to louse things up, and she'd pay the price.

But Jamie was already paying a price, a big one, for being here. Maybe Alison wasn't worth his concern, but he was the one who had to decide that.

"I'll do my best to get them to send a replacement for you." Mel wouldn't like it, and neither would Sharon. Meg would offer to pay the extra expense of sending a new person out. If going to bat for Jamie affected the project and her career took a hit, so be it. She waited for her tummy to start churning at the thought, but amazingly, it didn't.

Maybe the serendipity of meeting Clint had given her new respect for going with the flow. Maybe this country was beginning to have an effect on her priorities. Even that thought would ordinarily scare her to death, but she felt calm. If Jamie needed to go home to be with Alison, she'd support him.

"You'd really be okay with that?" Jamie gazed at her and seemed to make a valiant attempt to focus.

"I know how important she is to you." She smiled at him. "I hope someday to dance at your wedding."

"I hope to dance at our wedding, too." He shook his head. "Need coffee. Gotta go on the Net, get a ticket."

"Stay right here a minute. I'll find someone who can take you back to the ranch. But, Jamie, they can't get a replacement here in time for tomorrow morning. The three finalists and I are supposed to be on horseback for the broadcast, and I'm already nervous about it."

"Don't fret, Megster." Jamie rubbed her arm. "I'll do the gig and get us to Phoenix." His grin was crooked. "It's not like you can fly outta Sonoita, ya know."

"True." She glanced up when she saw a movement by the door. Clint was standing there looking worried. She beckoned him over. "Jamie needs to fly back to New York tomorrow," she said.

"What's wrong?"

"Family emergency." At least she hoped someday Alison would be family for Jamie.

Clint's worried frown deepened. "I hope nobody has di—"

"No, we're not talking about anything life-threatening. But he has to go home right away. I'm going to ask for a replacement first thing in the morning. I'll need to get up about five so I can call the studio and start the process." She looked into his eyes, and knew he was remembering the chaotic morning they'd had because of oversleeping.

"Right. I'll make sure you have an alarm clock."

"Need a ride to the ranch," Jamie mumbled. "Gotta get on the Net."

Clint looked confused. "What?"

"He wants to sober up and buy his ticket on the Internet," Meg said. "So he has to go back to the Circle W."

"I'll take him. I'll make him some coffee and let him use my computer."

It was the best solution. If she told anyone else they were free to take Jamie back, they'd know they weren't a finalist. But Meg hated to have Clint leave. She'd become used to the idea that he'd be there all evening and take her home.

"Thanks," she said, ignoring her own disappointment. "That would be wonderful."

"You'd better get in there," he said. "They're all asking for you."

"I will." She stood. "See you later."

"Right. Later."

She hurried toward the bar, but her heart was with Clint as he helped Jamie up and started toward the door. If she was this broken up over losing his company for the evening, how could she possibly give him up forever? He'd have to go along with her plan to be part of the contest as Meg's Pick. By doing that, he had a good chance to save his ranch, and they could find a way to merge their worlds. It was the only option she could see.

12

CLINT WAS GLAD for a chance to escape from the bar. He didn't know how Meg could deal with a mob scene like that on a regular basis. She was probably used to it, but Clint liked his social interaction to be with a handful of people, at most. One-on-one was his favorite.

And yeah, he was jealous of all the time she was giving to that crowd, and he had no right to be. She was here to see and be seen, not to hide away in a bedroom having sex with him. Anyone who ended up with Meg would have to take whatever spare time she had and be grateful.

"I 'preciate this, man," Jamie said as Clint gave him a boost up into the truck. "I promise not to barf on your seat."

"Don't worry about it." But Clint rolled the window down before he closed the door and went around to the driver's side. The cool air should help sober Jamie up, even if he didn't need to heave out the window. And having Jamie burp on his truck was better than hanging around watching guys drool over Meg. He climbed in and started Esmerelda's motor.

"She's okay, that Megster," Jamie said.

Clint had no argument with that. "Yeah, she's great."

"She doesn't want me t' leave."

"Probably not, but if you have an emergency—"

"Alison found a new guy."

Clint did a mental double take. He had to assume Alison was Jamie's girlfriend, but the situation didn't sound like much of an emergency. "That's why you're leaving?"

"Yep. Nip this in the bud."

Clint didn't get it. Bringing a replacement out here would certainly create problems for Meg. Surely she outranked Jamie, so she should be able to demand that he stay with her, even if his girlfriend had taken off with another man.

He'd pictured Meg as being focused on her goal, ready to do whatever it took to keep her spot on the show. Going along with Jamie didn't fit. "Were you and Alison engaged?" he asked.

"Not yet. But she's the one. It'll happen."

From the look of things, Jamie might be the only person who thought so. Clint was astounded that Meg was buying into this program. Then he remembered her saying that she felt sorry for the cowboys she didn't choose. Apparently she had a soft heart. He wasn't sure she could afford that if she wanted to keep her job.

"Meg's a good friend," Jamie said. "The best."

Clint had no business getting involved, but he couldn't help himself. "Won't this make things tough for her, switching cameramen after the whole thing's started?"

Jamie didn't say anything for a while. "Are you thinkin' I should stick around?"

"I don't know about that. But it's not Meg's fault that your girlfriend got involved with somebody else. Seems like she shouldn't have to suffer for it. She's just out here trying to do her job."

More silence from the passenger side of the cab. "I s'pose you're right," Jamie said at last. "But I don't wanna lose Alison."

"Buddy, you can't force these things." Clint did his best to be patient. Love was a hell of a thing to contend with. "Either it's right or it's not. Sometimes you just have to let go."

Jamie leaned his head back against the seat. "I wanna get married. I want kids. It's time."

"I know what you mean." And the funny thing was, Clint hadn't had such thoughts until recently, like yesterday, in connection with a very unlikely candidate. A guy didn't settle down with a woman like Meg. He could only grab hold and go along for a wild ride.

He pulled the truck in front of the house. "Here we are. Need help getting out?" If Jamie was starting to sober up, and Clint thought he was, he wouldn't appreciate being babied.

"I can make it." Jamie spoke with the careful enunciation of someone who was smashed and didn't want to seem smashed.

"Okay. Then I'll go in and make us a pot of coffee. Come on when you're ready."

"Thanks. I'll be in…shortly."

Clint headed into the house and left the front door ajar so Jamie wouldn't have too much to contend with. He had the coffee perking away when Jamie showed up in the kitchen, pale but not quite as wobbly.

"Have a seat." Clint motioned to a small table in the corner of the kitchen. "Unless you want to go into my office and get on the Internet while the coffee's brewing."

Jamie sat down on one of the scarred oak kitchen chairs and propped his head in his hands. "I'm still thinkin' about it."

Clint nodded and pulled a couple of mugs out of the cupboard. If he could keep Jamie from buying a ticket home until he'd sobered up completely, he might not do it at all. Clint thought the urge to run home had more to do with alcohol than good sense.

When the coffee finished brewing, he poured two mugs full and took them over to the table. "You take anything in it?"

"Nope. Thanks." Jamie blew across the surface of the coffee and took a sip. Then he choked.

"You okay?" Clint started to get up.

"Sit, sit." Jamie stopped him with his hand, then coughed and cleared his throat. "Some coffee, pardner."

"I like it strong."

"No shit. You could pave your driveway with this."

"Want me to water it down?"

"No, I'm gonna drink it. I'll bet it brings brain cells back from the dead."

"Maybe." Clint smiled as he picked up his mug. "And you killed off a bunch tonight."

"Yeah." Jamie seemed lost in thought as he slowly drank his coffee. When he finished the first cup, he got up and poured himself a second, and he seemed steadier. When that was gone, he put the empty mug on the table. "I'll stay."

Clint met his gaze. "Good."

"Thanks for keeping me from making a complete ass of myself. I guess Meg would've let me."

"She didn't like seeing you suffer."

"No, she didn't." Jamie turned his mug around and around. "She acts tough, but underneath she's a real softie." His words were distinct, as if time and caffeine had cleared the cobwebs.

"I believe you."

"Not many people know that. I sometimes think—ah, never mind." Jamie waved a hand in the air.

"What?"

"She'd kill me if she knew I'd said this, so don't tell her."

"I won't."

Jamie gazed across the table at him. "I know you won't. You're a real straight shooter, and that's a good thing. For what it's worth, I think it stinks that George, who's clueless, owns this ranch."

"Thanks."

"Anyway, back to Meg. In my humble opinion, she needs somebody she can be herself with. Most of the time she has to act invincible. I'm probably one of the few people she lets down her guard in front of. She can't even do that with her family. They're just waiting for her to fail so they can say I told you so."

Clint hated hearing that. He wanted her to be surrounded with people who wished her well. "Do you think she's in danger of getting kicked off the show?"

"I hope not, but this is a fickle business. You're golden one minute, crapola the next. That's another reason I wish she had somebody special, somebody who could cushion the blows."

Clint had to say it. "What about you?"

Jamie laughed. "Believe it or not, she's not my type. I go for rounder women, ones who like to cook and eat." He sighed. "Like Alison."

Now Clint felt guilty. "Look, if you think going back there is the answer, then I don't want to be the one who talked you out of it. I don't know her, and I barely know you. Forget what I said."

Jamie shook his head. "It's not the answer, and Meg needs me here. When I get back in two weeks I'll find out what's going on. But if I ran back there now, I'd look like a pathetic loser. You steered me right. I appreciate it. If there's anything I can ever do for you, let me know."

"Okay." Clint couldn't think of anything, but it was nice to know someone close to Meg was on his side.

Jamie stood. "Guess I'll head on down to the bunkhouse and do some editing. Are you going back to the Steak Out?"

"Probably not."

"Not your scene, huh?"

Clint shrugged, not wanting to put down something that might be a way of life for Jamie.

"I'm getting sick of the bar crowd, myself," Jamie said. "When I was twenty-five, getting loud and crazy in public was my main form of entertainment. Now that I'm pushing thirty, I'd rather have dinner by candlelight at home."

"I have to admit I like that, too." And he'd had a recent experience with just such a dinner and it had been outstanding.

"The thing about restaurants is that you have to drive home before you can…well, you know."

"Uh-huh."

"And Alison makes the most amazing Alfredo sauce…. Ah, I'm not going to think about Alison's Alfredo sauce, or anything else about her, or I'll be ready to hit the bottle again."

Clint wanted to ask if Jamie knew what kind of evening Meg liked best, but asking wouldn't be a good idea. Besides, it didn't matter. Her career choice meant she had to make a bunch of public appearances, whether she liked that or not. Quiet dinners would be few and far between for her.

"Are you planning to wait up for Meg?" Jamie asked.

He thought fast and came up with a reasonable explanation for doing that. "Yeah, probably. I wanted to talk to her about the horseback-riding plan for tomorrow."

"She's scared of horses. I'll bet that witch Mona knows it and talked Mel into the horse thing."

"I'll find her the equivalent of a rocking chair." Clint wished there had been time today to get her out there and acclimate her to the experience.

"She'll still be scared, but at least I won't have to worry about her, now that I know you're on top of it. If you're awake, would you tell her for me I've decided not to go back to New York?"

"Sure."

"Tell her it was the booze talking, and I've come to my senses. Hell, you'll know what to tell her. And thanks again."

"Any time." Clint flipped on the back porch light so that Jamie wouldn't have any trouble finding his way to the bunkhouse. A light was on down in the main room, probably Tuck reading one of his Westerns. Tuck wasn't much of a barfly, either, so he'd chosen to stay home tonight.

Tuck would keep Jamie company for the rest of the night, which relieved Clint of the job. He'd wondered if Jamie would decide to camp out in the house, maybe even choose to sleep on the sofa. That would have ended Clint's plans for some time alone with Meg.

Thinking of that, he made a quick trip to his bedroom and set the alarm clock for five. She might want to change it when she found out about Jamie, but he planned to advise her to get up at that time so they could go down to the barn and get acquainted with the horse she'd be on.

With that chore out of the way, he returned to the kitchen, poured himself another cup of coffee and walked into the living room. Damn, but it was quiet. He used to love solitude more than anything, but tonight the room lacked something...some*one*, to be more exact. Meg couldn't possibly have become that important to him in such a short time, could she?

With a sigh, he plopped down in his favorite chair and picked up a magazine. He hoped she'd get home soon. Then he mentally corrected that. He hoped she'd get *back* soon. This was his home, not hers. He needed to keep the reality of the situation firmly in mind or somebody might get hurt. And it would probably be him.

MEG CHOSE to ride back to the Circle W with Jed because she wanted to make sure he wasn't too disappointed about not getting on the show. "It was very hard to choose," she told him as they drove down the deserted highway.

"I'm sure."

"You are all awesome at your job." And they were party animals, too. Back at the Steak Out the celebration was still in full swing. When she'd mentioned that she needed to leave because of her early broadcast, she'd had a ton of offers to take her back, and she'd picked Jed. He had the added appeal of having consumed the fewest beers of anyone.

"I didn't think I'd make the finals." Jed chuckled and patted his stomach. "Too much good living and not enough crunches. But I'm happy for Denny. He'll have fun. Me, I would've been too nervous. I just entered because everybody was doing it and I didn't want to look like a wuss."

"Anybody who can eat a jar of those jalapeños is no wuss. I had one and my mouth was on fire. Do you eat those all the time?"

"Not like I did tonight. Everybody was showing off for you, me included. Besides, it helps if you drink beer. Water doesn't cool your mouth like beer."

"Too bad for me, I'd decided to lay off for tonight. I wanted to stay sharp for when I made the announcement about the finalists. And it was killing me because those margaritas looked delicious."

Jed nodded. "They're great margaritas. You'll have to come back when you can relax and enjoy one."

"I'd like that." If Clint went for her plan, she would be back for sure. The Circle W just might become her home away from home.

"I'll bet there are a lot of things you can't do that you want to."

"Some, but I try to look at the big picture." Right now her big picture included a certain lanky cowboy. All he had to do was agree to step into the frame.

Jed pulled his truck up in front of the ranch house. "Sit right there. I'll get your door."

"Jed, that's not necessary." She took quick note of the living-room windows and noticed the lights were still on. Her heart rate sped up.

"I think it's necessary." He hopped out, surprisingly agile for such a hefty guy. "If I'm going to tell this story, I want to make sure I come off as a gentleman."

She waited until he walked around and swung open the passenger door. When he held out his hand, she put hers into it and allowed him to help her down. "Thank you, kind sir."

His smile flashed in the darkness. "Thank you for letting me be the one to drive you home. The other guys were all ready to string me up when you did that. They'll pounce on me the minute I get back and demand every last detail."

"You're going back?"

"Are you kidding? I'm going back to gloat, man! Come on, I'll walk you to the door."

Meg laughed. "Then let the record show that I took your arm as we walked up the steps."

"All *right*."

"And kissed you on the cheek before you left." She gave him a quick peck.

"Wow. Now I'll have to quit shaving so I preserve that spot exactly as it is. Did you leave any lipstick?"

Meg checked and saw a faint lip print. "Yep. You have evidence."

"Cool." He reached for the screen door. "Let's make sure ol' Clint left the place open for you." He twisted the knob. "Looks like he did."

Excitement surged through her as she thought of Clint inside waiting for her. And she knew he would be. "Then I'll say goodnight."

"Same to you, ma'am." Jed touched the brim of his hat and charged down the steps, obviously bound for a moment of glory at the Steak Out.

Still smiling, Meg walked in the door. Clint sat in his easy chair, a magazine open on his lap. He glanced up with a slow, easy smile of welcome. She'd never seen anyone look so good in her life. She had the craziest feeling of homecoming, which made no sense. Or maybe it made incredible sense.

She closed the door and turned the lock. "Hey, you."

"Hi." He felt a rush of tenderness. She looked so damned good coming in the door of his house as if she owned the place. She was quickly taking possession of his heart, too, and he didn't know what to do about that, but he couldn't seem to stop the process.

She walked toward him. "Did Jamie get his ticket?"

"No. He decided not to go."

"Not to go?" She eased down to the sofa across from him. "Why not?"

Clint closed the magazine and tossed it on the coffee table. "After he had some coffee and thought it through, he realized that might not be the best answer to the problem."

Relief made her smile. She hadn't looked forward to engineering a substitution. "Your coffee would give anybody a come-to-Jesus moment."

"I'll have you know he had a second cup."

"So where is he now? Running laps around the corral?"

"Down at the bunkhouse editing. He asked me to give you the message that he'd changed his mind."

She gazed at him. "Why do I have the feeling that you influenced that decision?"

"I don't know that I did."

"I do." She stood. "And thank you." She held out both hands to him. "Is there some way I can show my appreciation?"

He drank in the sight of her standing there offering herself. She might never cross his path again, but for tonight, she wanted him, wanted to be with him until the morning tore them apart. He got up and took her hands in his. "Yes, ma'am, there certainly is."

13

BACK IN HIS BEDROOM, Clint took his time undressing Meg. Each time before, she'd started the festivities naked, but not tonight. And that seemed to fit, because he was a heck of a lot more coordinated about the process now. Twenty-four hours ago he'd been too intimidated and eager. His undressing technique would have left much to be desired. Tonight he was in control.

She'd worn her fringed black jacket, which he took off first. Underneath, she'd exchanged the blue-knit top she'd worn in the morning for a white spangled cowgirl shirt with pearl buttons at the wrists and down the front. He unfastened the snaps at her wrists first and kissed each pulse point.

"I like that," she murmured. "I didn't know I was sensitive there."

"Neither did I." He drew back her sleeve and ran his tongue from her wrist to the inside of her elbow.

"*Mmm.*"

"Good feedback." He repeated the caress on her other arm, moving slowly, enjoying the taste of her skin, the scent of soap and perfume.

She began to tremble. "Maybe…maybe it's the anticipation, but feeling your tongue there…I'm going a little crazy inside."

"Good." He gently unfastened the first three snaps of her blouse as he gazed into her eyes. "I want you to imagine me licking you…everywhere."

She took a shaky breath. "What do you suppose I've been thinking about ever since our shower?"

"This?" He left the rest of the snaps and unhooked the front catch of her bra. Then he slipped both hands inside to cradle her warm breasts. Her nipples tightened in response.

"Yes."

In one motion he peeled her bra and her blouse from her shoulders. She lifted her arms free. In that moment she transformed herself into an image of sexual abandon, half her clothes hanging loose around her and her breasts uncovered.

His groin grew hot and heavy as he gazed at her. He hadn't thought she could look any sexier with clothes than without, but this partial nudity made him want her in a fierce and untamed way.

"I love that wild look in your eyes." She cradled her breasts. "As if you could eat me up."

His mouth went dry. By touching her breasts, she'd tapped into an unrecognized fantasy of his. He covered her hands with his and leaned down to run his tongue along the curve of her finger as it pressed against her silken skin.

She brushed her thumb across her nipple, making it quiver. With a groan he took charge of that sweet nipple, rolling it against the roof of his mouth as tension pushed him closer to the breaking point.

"I need you," she murmured, her voice urgent. "Now. Right now."

He lifted his head, his body pulsing with the urge to be inside her. "I…meant to…go slow."

"Next time."

"Next time." Snaps popped, zippers rasped, and he pushed her down crossways on the bed without taking off his boots, without taking off his jeans.

Once his aching penis was free, he grabbed a condom and put it on. Then he lifted her hips and hooked her ankles over his shoulders. Knees braced against the mattress, he pushed deep and began thrusting.

They both came instantly, as if they'd had hours of foreplay. He'd never known a drive this strong. It left his brain spinning and his body out of control.

Gradually their breathing evened out, and the room came back into focus. Ending the magical connection, he gently lowered her back to the mattress. While he climbed out of the rest of his clothes, she slid under the covers. Finally he joined her there, gathering her close and kissing her with gratitude in his heart.

"Has it only been one day that we've known each other?" he asked, awestruck by the powerful emotions between them.

"One day, but two nights." She rested her head on his shoulder and hugged him close. "Clint, we have to do something about this situation."

He pretended not to know what she meant, because he had no solutions. "What situation?"

"You, me, fireworks."

"I only can think of one thing."

"What's that?" She sounded hopeful.

"You'll have to take some ugly pills. And maybe if you smelled a little more like a garbage dump and less like a field of flowers, and wore baggy clown outfits and a rubber nose, that would help, too."

She laughed. "Look, it's not all up to me. You're the one

who put on those sexy boots. And the fit of those jeans should be illegal. We won't even mention what a hottie you become when you wear your hat. So don't think I'm taking all the blame for this fiasco."

"Hey, I tried to avoid the cowboy thing. I didn't wear any of that stuff when you first got here."

She sighed. "True. And I still craved your body."

"And I've craved yours from the beginning. It's a problem." He kept his tone light, but the subject was anything but. And no answer in sight.

"Clint, there is a solution."

"Yeah, yeah." He tweaked her nose. "Even if you begged me, I can't see you wearing a chastity belt. That's a definite no."

"I mean a real solution. Take part in the contest."

"Huh?" He readjusted their position so her head was on the pillow. Then he propped himself on his elbow because he needed to look into her eyes and try to figure out what craziness was going through her mind. "Too much sex must be frying my brain, because I don't get how that ties in with anything. For one thing, the Arizona contest is over."

"Yes, and there wasn't time to get you into the regular competition, so I called the studio this afternoon. I have permission to add a wild-card contestant at any time. He'll be called Meg's Pick, and the slot would go to you."

"Hey, hey, wait a minute. I don't want to be—"

"Let me finish. I wouldn't have to announce it right away. In fact, I should probably wait until all the state contests are finished. We're talking about another thirteen days."

"I thought you knew how I felt about this contest." The longer she talked, the less he felt listened to. She was ignoring everything he'd told her about himself and that didn't feel good.

"I know it wouldn't be easy for you, but think of the end result. You would have a reason to be in New York." She paused. "I'll be in New York."

He knew that. It was part of the problem. "And the contest stuff would last how long—a few days? I don't think buying us a few days is worth what you're asking."

"I'd say more than a few days. Once you're on TV, all sorts of opportunities would come your way, even if you didn't win. Endorsements, guest appearances—you'd be in demand for months. Some of the work might be in L.A., but a good part of it would be in New York."

He couldn't think of anything he'd hate more. "Meg, that's not my thing. I've tried to tell you that." His disappointment grew. She didn't know him at all.

"But think of what this would mean! You could earn all kinds of money, maybe even enough to buy back the Circle W!"

"You're asking me to prostitute myself so I can maybe buy this place? Sorry, the price is too high."

Her expression became stormy. "Come on, now, Clint. It wouldn't be that bad."

"Easy for you to say. It's your world. You feel comfortable there. I would feel like a trained bear in a circus."

"I don't believe that. And you don't really know, because you've never tried it. And…and yes, it's my world. I…thought I could share a part of it with you."

"Then I guess you just don't get me." He'd felt so warm a moment ago, and now cold was creeping relentlessly through him, chilling his soul. "If you could imagine I'd want to do something like that, you don't have the first idea of who I am."

She clenched her jaw. "Just like that, you'd give up a

chance to earn a pile of money and be with me at the same time?"

"Like I said, the price is too high."

"I must have misunderstood." She cleared the huskiness from her throat. "I thought the ranch meant a lot to you."

"It does."

"Then how are you ever going to buy it back? Winning the lottery isn't a plan, Clint!"

"I know that. So I'm racing a quarterhorse next season. Gabriel's got talent, and once he starts winning, the money will be there. It might take a couple of years, but—"

"And me? How do I fit into all that? I thought…I meant something to you."

"You do."

"But not enough." Her lower lip quivered.

"Not enough to compromise who I am."

"I don't see it that way." She blinked away tears.

"Meg, I'm sorry. It wouldn't work. I appreciate the thought, but—"

"No, you don't." She sat up and swung her legs over the edge of the bed. "You don't appreciate it, you hate it. You're insulted that I would ask it of you."

He sat up, too. "Okay, I do think it shows that you don't understand me, and that's disappointing."

"I understand that you're so set in your ways that you won't compromise, not even to get what you say you want." She walked around to the other side of the bed and gathered up her clothes.

"Meg, I don't want us to end like this."

She held the bundle of clothes against her like a shield. "I didn't want us to end at all. I wanted to find a way that we could keep seeing each other. To know that you're ready to give up—well, that hurts." She turned and walked out of the room.

"Wait! You don't have an alarm clock!"

Her voice floated back to him. "Don't worry. I won't need one."

With a groan, he flopped back onto the mattress and stared up at the beamed ceiling. Dammit, why couldn't she understand? Why did she have to imply that if he really cared about her, he'd parade around in front of a TV camera?

If she really cared about him, she'd never ask. It seemed as if she was trying to turn him into a different kind of guy. He could keep the cowboy outfit, but underneath that she wanted a more sophisticated man, one who moved in the same circles she did. She didn't really want him the way he was.

Endorsements and public appearances. The concept gave him hives. Even if he wanted to do it for her sake, he didn't think he could. He wasn't cut out to be in the limelight.

But she was. She'd found her calling, and he'd found his. And the two were totally incompatible. As perfectly as their bodies meshed, their lives were exact opposites and always would be that way.

He should probably consider himself lucky for what they'd shared. He should, but he didn't. After the kind of loving he'd had with Meg, anything else would be a joke. He'd always expected to marry some day, but Meg might have spoiled him for another woman. And, God help him for being such a selfish bastard, but he hoped he'd spoiled her for another man.

MEG TOOK cat naps throughout the night. She was too exhausted to stay awake and too upset to stay asleep. When she'd conceived her plan, she hadn't considered that Clint might say no.

Between his love of the Circle W and his obvious attraction to her, he had two strong reasons to agree. She hadn't expected him to be crazy about the idea, but she had expected him to be willing to give it a shot. After all, she'd eliminated any need for him to compete here on his home turf.

All he'd have to do was appear on TV. Surely even the most private guy in the world could do that if it meant getting everything he wanted as a result. Maybe he didn't care enough about her—and that stung—but the ranch had been in his family for generations. He could reclaim it now, instead of waiting around to see if his precious horse Gabriel won enough races.

The more she thought about his stubborn refusal to try, the angrier she became. Well, if he wanted to be a martyr, then let him. She was sorry that she'd ever become involved.

She was especially sorry because, stubborn and proud though he was, he'd given her the best climaxes of her life. Although she didn't have a huge basis of comparison, she had a hunch that sex like that didn't come along very often. She had enough problems in the dating arena already, without having Mr. Yummy Cowboy raise the bar to impossible heights.

Every time she woke up and remembered where she was, and who was right down the hall, she had to control the urge to make that trip. He would take her back into his bed, no question. She was the one who had called a halt.

But she'd had to do that once she'd known for sure he wouldn't make any effort to keep the relationship going when she so plainly wanted to. A girl had to preserve a little of her pride after being so resoundingly rejected. So she stayed in her room and checked her watch every time she opened her eyes.

Although she'd originally planned to get up at five, she'd decided six was soon enough now that Jamie was staying on. If she hadn't been so angry with Clint, she'd feel grateful that he'd apparently convinced Jamie not to leave. But she didn't have room in her heart for gratitude right now.

At five she heard a tap on the door. "I don't need to get up yet!" she called, irritated by a summons she didn't even need.

"Yes, you do. I want you to get dressed and come down to the barn with me."

Instantly her body reacted, yearning for a predawn rendezvous in the barn with Clint. She envisioned the two of them getting it on in the hay, their bodies hot and yearning, the earthy scent of the barn filling her nostrils, a climax building…. "I am not having barn sex with you! Of all the nerve!" *Beg me, plead with me and maybe I'll change my mind.*

There was a pause followed by the sound of him clearing his throat. "If you're planning to get on a horse today, I want you and the horse to become acquainted. Jamie said horses scare you."

Damn Jamie and his big mouth. "Not so much." And his suggestion had nothing to do with sex, which was a big disappointment.

"Meg, I know how much this broadcast means to you. And I know you don't want to give Mona the satisfaction of seeing you sitting up there frozen with fear. It'll show on camera, and you know it."

Unfortunately, he was right. "For a guy who never plans to be on TV, you sound like quite the authority."

"Okay. Suit yourself."

"Wait. Let me throw on some clothes." The thought of Mona snickering as she watched Meg paralyzed with fright on top of that horse was enough to overcome her reluctance.

"Tuck will probably be down there, too, so you don't have to worry about…anything."

"I'm not worried." Hopeful, but not worried. In spite of being furious with him, she still wanted him. Just the sound of his voice got her hot.

She searched her wardrobe and discovered she had nothing that fit the occasion. She'd expected to spend her time in the public eye, not down at the barn with Clint getting acquainted with a horse. After pulling on the plainest pair of cropped jeans she'd brought, she shoved her feet into a pair of denim slides and pulled a turtleneck sweater over her head.

All her jackets were too nice to risk getting chewed and covered with horse slobber. She'd seen enough cowboy movies to know that getting acquainted with a horse usually involved the horse chewing or drooling on something, probably the fringe on her black suede jacket. The sweater might be warm enough and was more horse-proof.

As she opened her bedroom door, the aroma of coffee greeted her. Clint's coffee. As rocky as she felt after so little sleep, she could use some. She walked into the kitchen to find him sipping from a mug.

He wore a white T-shirt that did wonders for his pecs, and another pair of wear-softened jeans that she thought ought to carry a warning label for susceptible females. His denim jacket with the lamb's-wool collar lay over the back of a kitchen chair.

He lowered the mug and gazed at her. A tense silence

stretched between them. "You'll need a jacket. It's cold out there."

She watched his lips as he spoke. "I'll be fine." She hoped someday she'd be able to forget about his wonderful mouth and all the pleasure it had given her.

"No, you won't. You'll freeze. But I can understand if you don't want to wear your nice ones." He put down his mug and picked up his jacket. "Take this. I'll get another one for me."

"Really, I'll be—"

"Take it, Meg." He thrust it toward her.

She decided not to argue and took the jacket. "Thanks. Can I...have some coffee?"

"I thought you didn't like it."

"I never said that. I only said it's strong. Strong is good, especially this morning."

He nodded, as if agreeing with her. "Help yourself. I'll be right back."

When he was gone she gave in to the temptation to bury her nose in the lamb's-wool collar of his coat. After breathing deeply, she sighed. Pure cowboy.

Then she hung the jacket around her shoulders while she opened cupboards until she found the mugs. There were a slew of them, all the same—thick, white, utilitarian. Ranch-house mugs.

She poured herself a cup of Clint's ranch-house coffee and knew she would miss this place, in addition to missing the man who lived here. The simplicity of living out in the middle of nowhere had more appeal than she could have imagined.

She'd been appalled to discover Sonoita had no department stores, but she'd never once had the urge to shop. She'd worried about the lack of TV reception, and except

for the basketball game on the sets in the bar the night before, she'd seen no television and hadn't missed it.

The coffee smelled wonderful when she lifted the mug
to her lips. It tasted like desire—hot, thick and pungent.
Clint made love the same way he brewed coffee.

He walked in wearing a lined flannel shirt over his
white T-shirt. "How's the coffee?"

"Perfect." She took another swallow.

He came over to get his mug, and she decided not to
move away, although having him close made her heart
pound. She was still angry with him, but that didn't mean
she'd lost the urge to kiss him. If he felt the same, he deserved to be tortured by having her close by.

He picked up his mug and closed his eyes as he swallowed a mouthful of coffee. Then he opened them again
and lifted the mug in her direction. "You can bring your
coffee if you want. We should probably get on down
there."

"Okay." She put the mug on the counter and shoved her
arms in the sleeves of the jacket. They hung a good two
inches below the tips of her fingers.

"Here. Let me fix that." Clint put down his mug,
grabbed a sleeve and started rolling it up.

She'd maintained control until that moment, until his
fingers brushed her skin and she remembered how his
tongue had felt on the inside of her arm. Her tummy
clenched and she began to quiver.

If he noticed, he gave no indication. After finishing with
one sleeve, he began rolling up the other. She had trouble
getting her breath. She wanted him so much she couldn't
see straight.

"There." He seemed to avoid looking at her deliberately
as he turned to pick up his mug again while she did the

same. At the door he grabbed his hat off a peg and settled it on his head. "Let's go."

It was still dark outside as they made their way by the glow of the back porch light down the hill to the corrals. Meg's toes quickly felt like ice cubes, and she wished she had real boots instead of the trendy shoes she'd brought. But inside Clint's denim jacket, she was snug and warm.

She wondered what it would be like to dress for warmth and comfort instead of catering to fashion all the time. She'd always told herself that updating her wardrobe was a fun part of being a celebrity, but she was a little tired of the pressure to look good. Days off now and then wouldn't be a bad thing.

She held Clint's coffee mug for him while he opened the heavy barn door. When he took it back their hands brushed, but again he didn't seem to take any notice of it. Inside the barn he switched on a light.

The scent of horses, hay and leather swirled around Meg. She felt vaguely uneasy, but having Clint next to her helped. The barn had six stalls on each side, and the first two were empty.

Horses immediately popped their heads over the stall doors of the other ten. They gazed eagerly toward Clint and a couple of them nickered a greeting. Tuck was no-where around.

"Not quite chow time yet," Clint said. "But I guess we can give each of you a little early-morning snack." He drained his coffee cup and set it down on a ledge just inside the door.

Meg followed suit. She wasn't sure what he expected of her, but she'd probably need both hands.

He picked up a bucket and took off the lid. Inside was something that looked like uncooked oatmeal. He held the bucket toward her. "Take a handful of oats. You can feed a handful to each one of them."

"With my hand? Won't they bite me?"

"No." He picked up a handful and held his palm flat, the oats in the middle of his palm. "Especially if you do it like this."

"I...I've never fed a horse before."

Clint smiled at her, not a trace of animosity in his gaze. "Come on, Meg. Considering how fast you had me eating out of your hand, these horses should be no challenge at all."

A curl of sexual tension twisted inside her. "I don't have you eating out of my hand anymore, now do I?"

"That's what you think. No matter how much I tell myself to leave well enough alone, all I want to do is grab you and kiss you all over."

14

CLINT KNEW HE probably shouldn't have admitted that, but Meg looked so sad and vulnerable that he'd wanted to bring some color to her cheeks. His comment must have worked, because now she sparkled again.

She gazed at him as if she'd like nothing better than to have him kiss her all over. "Thanks for saying that."

"I can't do it, though."

"I know."

"Tuck could be along any minute. He wouldn't tell anyone, but…"

"It's better if no one knows." She hesitated. "Especially if you should change your mind about the contest."

"I won't," he said, as gently as he could. "I'm sorry."

Her chin lifted, and her brown eyes gleamed with the kind of determination that had probably gotten her where she was today. "I think you will be sorry, in the long run. I think you're making a huge mistake, which is why I want to leave the door open. You can notify me anytime between now and the day we bring the finalists on the show."

"Meg, it's not going to happen. You'd be better off forgetting about it."

Her spine straightened even more. "Don't worry about me, Clint. I'll be so busy I won't have time to think about you. You're the one with the front porch you love to sit on and the far horizon you love to stare at. Maybe during one of those times you'll figure out that you're being an idiot."

"Fair enough." He watched her cover her vulnerability with a virtual suit of armor. No matter how necessary that process was, he hated to see it happen. Jamie thought she needed to allow someone past that barrier. Clint had been that special someone for a while, a very short while, but he wasn't that person anymore.

She reached for a handful of oats. "Do the horses like this?"

"They love it. The bay on the right here is Gabriel."

"The wonder horse who will save the ranch?"

To her credit, she didn't sound the slightest bit sarcastic. He appreciated that more than she knew. "I hope so."

"Then he definitely needs treats. Have some oats, Gabriel." She edged toward the stall and stretched out her hand, palm open.

Gabriel had to crane his neck to nibble at the oats, and Meg gasped when the horse's mouth snuffled against her palm, but soon the oats were gone.

Meg turned to him in triumph. "I did it! More oats!"

As the keeper of the oats, he followed her from stall to stall. Each time she grew braver, and finally, with a chestnut gelding named Prince, she took a giant step and stroked his nose.

"That's the horse you'll be on during the broadcast," Clint said. He'd deliberately had her finish up with Prince, hoping that by the time she fed Prince his oats, she'd be relaxed enough to enjoy the experience.

"Prince has nice eyes," she said.

"He's a gentleman. You'll be safe."

She inched closer to the stall and leaned on the door so

she could rub Prince's silky neck. "You must think I'm a real 'fraidy cat."

He tried not to feel jealous of Prince. "You didn't grow up with horses. That changes everything."

"No, I didn't, and when I was a little girl I got in the way of one of New York City's finest riding a very big horse during a parade. Or it seemed like a big horse to a four year old. It was my fault that I was knocked down, but I was terrified of that horse, and all horses afterward."

"That's too bad." If he had time, he could cure her of that. She'd already come a long way. But after this contest she'd probably never be in close contact with a horse again, so what was the point?

Even so, the horseman in him wanted to build on what they'd accomplished. "If you think there's time, we could take Prince out of the stall and I could boost you up on his back."

"With no saddle?" Fear crept back into her eyes.

"Sure. I actually like bareback riding better. You get a good feel for the horse that way."

"Uh..." She glanced at her watch. "I really should get up to the house and change. I don't want a repeat of yesterday."

He didn't want to push her, and she'd probably be fine for the broadcast now that she'd met and touched her horse. "Okay. Go on. I'll stay here and get Prince ready for his closeup." That way he wouldn't be in the house during the dangerous time she'd be naked in the shower.

"All right." She walked over to the door and picked up their empty mugs. "See you soon."

He glanced down at her feet. "I don't suppose you have any normal shoes."

"These are normal."

"Not out here." But he didn't want to make her nervous by implying her shoes would be a problem. After all, she'd only be sitting there, not riding around. "Never mind. Those will work."

"Good." She sounded relieved. "I want this to go very smoothly today."

"Don't worry. Prince won't let you down."

PRINCE WOULDN'T let her down, Meg told herself later on as she started back toward the barn. But Prince's owner might. If he'd been awake most of the night, too, then he'd had plenty of time to think. And thinking had produced no positive results, judging from his unchanged attitude about the contest.

So, she'd concentrate on her job. This morning she felt much more together. She'd dressed in a red suede vest over a black Western shirt paired with tight black cropped jeans. And red suede slides.

She hoped her shoes were okay for this gig. The red slides matched the vest, which was why she'd bought them. She'd never expected to get on a horse, though.

As she descended the hill, she could see that Jamie was nearly organized for their time on the bird. He'd clapped his earphones on and the huge antenna sprouted from the roof of the live truck, ready to grab satellite time. The umbrella lights were in position and all three finalists—Denny, Bill and a cute Latino from Nogales named Carlos—were mounted up. Knowing how efficient Jamie was, no doubt they were miked up, too.

Clint stood to one side holding Prince by the reins. In spite of feeding Prince a handful of oats this morning, Meg felt a clutch of fear at the thought of climbing aboard that giant animal. A little pony would have suited her better.

Then she grimaced as she imagined what Mona would have to say if Meg showed up riding a little horse. No, Prince was the right choice, and Clint had promised everything would go fine. She trusted him in that respect.

She hadn't written a script for this morning because the sequence was so straightforward. First she'd praise all the contestants and describe how difficult the choice had been. Then she'd introduce each finalist and ask a few questions. Finally she'd devote a minute or so to thanking the people of Sonoita for being such wonderful hosts, plug the next episode taking place in Kremmling, Colorado, and they'd be out of time.

This morning's broadcast had brought an even bigger crowd of bystanders, and Tuck had them rounded up over by the corral, away from the action. If time allowed, Meg thought it would be fun to have Jamie pan the crowd while everyone waved. That move usually pleased everyone, from the producers in the studio to the bystanders getting a brief taste of fame.

She smiled and called out a greeting to the knot of onlookers under Tuck's supervision. Their response was more enthusiastic than yesterday morning. Most of them had been at the Steak Out, and now they felt a personal connection with her.

She felt the same about them. In some ways she envied them being a part of this tight little community. She'd bet more people lived in her New York apartment building than in Sonoita, and yet the connections here were so much stronger.

Before she could climb aboard Prince, she had to attach her own mike and make sure Jamie knew the game plan. And she needed to give him a hug and thank him for hanging in there with her.

Because of the cables running everywhere, he was obviously worried about the men on horseback getting tangled up. And of course the finalists had chosen lively horses to show off their skills. Thank goodness she had Prince, who stood off to the side, head lowered, eyes closed.

She hoped he perked up a little for the broadcast, though. She didn't want Prince to look like a nag on TV. Maybe Clint would have a suggestion about how to get Prince to look lively for five minutes.

In the meantime, she had business with Jamie. She walked over and tapped him in the shoulder. "Hi, there."

He turned and smiled at her. "You look fabulous."

"Thanks. And thank you for deciding to stay on."

"Thank him." Jamie tipped his head in Clint's direction. "Between his cool head and killer coffee, I saw the error of my ways."

Meg laughed because she knew he expected her to, but her heart ached something fierce. Clint had been Jamie's friend—why couldn't he agree to be hers and enter the contest?

"So, you're—hold on a sec." Jamie winced and adjusted his earphones.

"Let me guess. The finalists are all tapping on their mikes."

"Yep. I've told them a dozen times that they're working, and they're live. They don't believe me and keep shouting into them. I'm going deaf." He glanced over at Prince. "So you're getting on that sorry-looking beast?"

"Prince is going to be magnificent."

Jamie raised his eyebrows. "A shot of Clint's coffee is what he needs. I'm hoping he doesn't decide to lie down in the middle of the segment."

"Good Lord, do you think he might?"

"No, no." Jamie rubbed her arm. "Not a chance. Didn't mean to worry you. Just kidding around."

"Don't kid around about horses."

"Right. Go get miked and climb aboard that hay-burner. We're getting close."

"I know." She leaned over and kissed Jamie on the cheek. "I don't know what I'd do without you."

"That's good, 'cause you're stuck with me, now. I'm even starting to like this Home on the Range routine."

"Me, too."

"You?" His mouth dropped open.

"Surprise, surprise." Then she walked over to the live truck to get her mike.

CLINT COULDN'T BELIEVE the chaos taking place on his peaceful ranch. Okay, it was George's ranch, now, but it was still Clint's in spirit. What an insane amount of racket. The Circle W hadn't been this noisy during branding.

Nostalgia gripped him. He missed those days more than he generally admitted. Mostly he tried to accept the situation as it was and live within the confines of reality. But he'd loved growing up on a working ranch and wished that his kids could do the same.

And here came the very woman he would love to have kids with. He pictured a couple of cute little carrot-tops running around, full of the devil, bound for glory. She'd teach those kids to go for what they wanted.

But her children would grow up in New York, and that was the sticking point. He sighed. He might imagine them chasing each other around this ranch, but it was total fan-

Meg stopped six feet away from Clint and Prince. "I need to get on," she said, not looking happy about it.

"Then you'll have to come a little closer, unless you're figuring on taking a flying leap into the saddle."

"Very funny." She took a deep breath and walked slowly up to Prince. "Anybody got a ladder?"

Clint looped the reins over Prince's neck and cupped his hands about three feet off the ground. "Put your foot right here, grab the saddle horn and I'll boost you up." She had on another pair of her ridiculous open-toed, backless shoes, but once she was in the saddle, it wouldn't matter.

"Will he stand right there while I do that?"

"He will."

She lifted her foot and placed it in his cupped hands. "I should have worn looser pants."

And he'd been trying so hard not to notice the snug fit. Now he couldn't help it. The way those pants outlined her tush made his mouth water.

"Here goes nothing." She swung up into the saddle and landed with a little thump.

Prince broke wind.

"Tell me he's not going to do that on camera," Meg wailed. "I'm sure they all heard that back at the studio and are killing themselves laughing."

"Yes, they are!" Jamie called over, a huge grin on his face. "They're loving the Megster on a musical horse. Okay, you two, bring that show on over here in front of the camera. We're live in five."

"Shove your feet in the stirrups," Clint said. "I'll lead you over there."

"It's hard in these shoes." Staring straight ahead, she kicked around, trying to feel for the stirrups, and almost lost a shoe.

"I'll do it." He positioned one foot in the stirrup and ducked under Prince's neck to get to the other side. Then he knotted the reins and handed them to her.

Her hand quivered as she took them.

"You okay?"

"I…guess so. I made the mistake of looking down while you fixed the stirrups. I'm really far off the ground. If he bucks me off…"

"He won't buck you off." He wanted to put a comforting hand on her knee, but he couldn't do that in front of everybody. He tried to get her to meet his gaze, but she was looking everywhere except at him. "You can do this, Meg," he said in a low voice. "Piece of cake."

"I don't know." Her glance darted here, there, everywhere, as if trying to find a way to escape.

"Look at me."

Finally she did.

"You'll be fine," he said, telegraphing confidence as best he could.

Some of the panic left her eyes. "Okay." She gulped softly. "Let's go."

After taking hold of the bridle, Clint started over toward Jamie, who waved them in like a guy on a tarmac berthing a jumbo jet.

"Good," Jamie said at last. "If you could lead the other three into position the same way, I'd appreciate it."

A chorus of groans from the finalists told Clint they didn't want to be led into position.

Jamie turned to them. "Trust me, you don't want one of those valuable animals getting crossways with some of this expensive equipment. All sorts of bad things could happen."

The guys muttered in protest, but Clint could see the

wisdom of having him act as a handler. He glanced up at Meg. "Hanging in?"

She nodded, although she had a white-knuckled grip on the saddle horn.

He hated to leave her, but Jamie was counting down the minutes. Clint brought Denny in first, because he trusted Denny and his horse, Slick, to behave themselves. He took Carlos and his pinto next, because the horse seemed less wild than Bill's crow-hopping Arab.

Finally he took hold of the bridle of Bill's horse and started over. "Be sure and keep a tight rein on him," he said.

"Spoilsport."

"I mean it, Bill. Meg's not used to horses. And like Jamie said, there's all kinds of valuable equipment here. Don't screw around." He wished he had more faith in Bill's good judgment.

"I'll be good, Mommy," Bill said as Clint led him into position beside Carlos.

"Okay, folks, ten seconds." Jamie glanced at Prince. "Meg's horse looks embalmed. Can we do anything about that?"

"Just tug on the reins a little, Meg," Clint said.

She lifted the reins, but if there was a tug, Clint couldn't tell. She was probably too afraid to give a real tug, in case something horrible might happen.

"Oh, well," Jamie said. "Five seconds." He held up his hand and counted silently down to one. Then he pointed at Meg.

Her smile bloomed. "Happy Trails, Mel and Mona! I'm here to introduce the three hottest cowboys in Arizona!"

Clint had to hand it to her. She was still scared to death, judging from the way she clutched the saddle horn, but she'd overridden that fear to put on a show for the camera. No doubt about it, she was a born performer.

Prince, unfortunately, was not. He looked bored by the entire thing. But Clint would rather have him standing there looking bored than moving around restlessly like the other three in the lineup.

Meg introduced Denny first, and then Carlos. By the time she got to Bill, his Arab was really starting to cut up. Clint thought Bill was egging the horse on for the effect. What a jerk.

"So, Bill," Meg asked, "what makes you special?"

"Meg, everything about me is special," Bill said. "Just ask Firebolt." On cue, his horse reared and pawed the air.

Jolted out of his doze, Prince threw back his head and hopped sideways. Meg screamed. In an instant, the lineup dissolved as horses plunged this way and that, with Denny and Carlos cussing a blue streak.

Clint dodged flailing hoofs to get to Meg, and somewhere in the process he lost his hat. But he managed to grab Prince's bridle and got a tight grip on the horse's nose, forcing him to stand quietly. "Easy, boy. Easy."

"We're done!" Jamie said. "Off the air! Guys, control those horses, or somebody's gonna get hurt. Maybe even by me. Bill, you're on my shit list, man. What a dumbass stunt."

Clint glanced up at Meg. She was gulping air, and makeup couldn't disguise that she'd gone white with terror. If Clint hadn't had his hands full, he would have cheerfully pulled Bill from his horse and beaten the tar out of him.

But Clint had more important things to do, like making sure this incident hadn't made Meg's fear worse. "You did great," he said. "You hung on."

She swallowed. "I didn't do great. I screamed. That made everything worse. I...I ruined the broadcast."

"No, Bill ruined the broadcast."

"Hey, nothing's ruined," Jamie said, walking toward them with his earphones around his neck. "I just got the word. Everyone loved it. The phones are going crazy." He picked up Clint's hat from the ground, dusted it off and handed it to him. "Mostly they loved you, buddy, the hero who leaped in to save Meg."

For the first time, Clint realized he'd appeared on camera. He'd been so desperate to help Meg that he hadn't even thought about it. Well, hell.

"America wants you in the running," Jamie said. "They want Bill dumped and you put in his place."

Clint stared up at Meg. She gazed back at him in silence, obviously unwilling to say anything to influence him.

Jamie clapped him on the shoulder. "What do you say? I mean, that was great TV. You could really capitalize on it."

Clint continued to gaze at Meg. "I'm sorry," he said. "I'm not interested."

15

MEG KEPT HERSELF busy until she and Jamie were packed up and ready to leave. Bill had apologized, and she'd decided to keep him as the third finalist. He'd get his trip to New York, but she could guarantee he wouldn't win. She'd talked to Sharon at the studio, and Bill was not popular with viewers.

Clint, however, was. Too bad. The guy couldn't see his way clear to go on the show, so that was that.

And they wouldn't be having a touching Hollywood goodbye, either. Half of Sonoita was standing around when she and Jamie walked out to the live truck, which Jamie had parked in front of the ranch house. Clint was there, too, but she didn't focus on him for fear that she would cry.

Instead she spent time saying goodbye to Tuck, Jed, José and Denny. She'd be seeing Denny in just over two weeks. Although Tuck had suggested she come back for a visit soon, she knew that wouldn't happen.

Finally she turned to Clint. "Thanks for being a good host." She held out her hand and allowed herself one more look into those gorgeous blue eyes.

He shook her hand briefly, and his gaze gave nothing away. "You're welcome. It was great having you here."

As a lump started to grow in her throat, she smiled and turned away. "Bye, everyone!" Then she jumped in the live truck before the waterworks started.

All the way to Phoenix, Jamie asked her what was wrong. She told him she'd caught a cold. She didn't think he bought it, but after a while he left her alone.

By tonight, they'd be in Colorado, and the process would start over. Somehow she'd have to pull herself together, because at the moment her on-camera persona didn't mesh with the way she felt inside. She was paid to be pert and bubbly. Instead she felt like a two-day-old glass of champagne. She wished she'd never laid eyes on Clint Walker.

CLINT HELD his act together until the white van pulled away from the house. Then he strode to the barn, saddled Nugget and headed out. He rode all afternoon, until darkness forced him back to the barn. Just his luck he ran into Tuck coming out of the barn.

"Where did you go off to?" Tuck asked. "I rode all over the place looking for you. I just came back a little while ago, myself."

"I had to clear my head after having the TV people here for two days," Clint said. "Is anything wrong?"

"I thought you'd want to know that the folks from Meg's station in New York called. They really want you on that show."

"They called here?" He'd thought it was over, now that Meg was gone. Obviously not. Maybe his life was screwed up for good.

"They called again because after finding out you turned them down, they want to give you a bonus if you'll appear on the show. They wouldn't tell me how much they're offering, of course. But they said you might want to consider getting yourself an agent."

Clint stared at his foreman. "An *agent?* Why the hell would I need an agent?"

"Don't bite my head off. I'm just the messenger."

"An agent!" Clint shook his head. "All I did was get Meg's horse calmed down!"

"According to the woman I talked to on the phone, I think her name's Sharon something-or-other, you made quite an impression doing that. I guess it was a real Kodak moment. They think you need an agent because you'll be fielding other calls, other offers."

"That's the craziest thing I've ever heard in my life." Clint undid the cinch on Nugget's saddle.

"So they've all gone home by now, but this Sharon person gave me her cell-phone number, and she said for you to call anytime. I suppose they stay up 'till all hours back there, but I thought you'd want to call before it got too late, with the time difference and all."

Clint pulled the saddle off and plopped it on a wooden rack by the door. "Tuck, I appreciate you taking the message, but I won't be calling her back. I have no intention of getting involved in any of it."

Tuck cleared his throat. "Uh, would that have anything to do with whatever went on between you and Meg?"

Clint whirled to face him. "Nothing went on between me and Meg."

"If you say so." Tuck gazed at him with a knowing expression.

"What…what do you think went on?"

"Well, I have no hard evidence, if that's what you mean. But I'd be willing to bet that the two of you got friendly while she was here. Jamie thought so, too."

Clint was dismayed to feel himself blushing. "We…um…it wasn't really…aw, hell, Tuck. It's over and done with now, anyway."

"Too bad."

"What do you mean *too bad?* She's a TV star, in case you haven't noticed. There's no room in her life for somebody like me."

"Or no room in your life for somebody like her?"

"She wanted to make me into a trained monkey. Can you picture me strutting around in front of a camera?"

Tuck rubbed his chin. "It's not so bad, once you get used to it."

Instantly Clint felt horrible for saying that. Tuck had been proud of his moments on TV, and Clint had made it sound like a ridiculous thing to do. "With you it was way different," he said. "She wasn't parading you out there as a contestant for the hottest cowboy. Your deal was more dignified."

Tuck burst out laughing. "Is that what's standing in the way of you taking those offers and making good money? Dignity?"

Clint was highly offended. "What if it is?"

Tuck shook his head. "It's a mighty high price to pay for dignity, if you ask me. You lose the money and the girl. I suspect you could stand both in your life." He started chuckling again. "Dignity. Lord Almighty."

"You don't understand." Clint felt as if the whole world had decided to beat up on him today.

"No, I probably don't. Probably too old."

"Besides, we don't need the money. Gabriel's going to come through for us."

Tuck sobered and glanced over toward Gabriel's stall. "That's something else we need to talk about."

A wave of uneasiness passed through Clint. "What do you mean?"

"Gabriel's favoring his left front foot. I think I've pushed him too hard, because I wanted him to be ready for the start of the season in Tucson. But he's young, and he'll be fine if we ease up."

"Ease up?" Clint didn't like the sound of that. "For how long?"

"Hard to say. But I can't promise you he'll race this spring. You could ruin him. I didn't want to bring this up until after we got through the TV deal, because I knew you'd be disappointed."

Disappointed wasn't the word. *Devastated* was more like it. Clint had been counting on Gabriel more than he'd thought. Now the horse was turning into an iffy proposition.

Tuck clapped him on the shoulder. "Don't worry too much about it. We'll see what the next few weeks bring." He looked toward the house. "Well, I think José's made cordon bleu for tonight, so I'm heading up for dinner. Should we set you a place at the table?"

Clint didn't feel like eating, but if he said no, that would confirm that he was either a lovesick fool or a guy who couldn't take bad news about his horse. So he'd eat dinner as usual and act as if everything was great. "Sure. I'll be right up."

After Tuck left, Clint turned to Nugget and reached up to scratch behind the horse's ears. "Too bad you're not a race horse, buddy. Without a race horse, I really will look like an idiot. But I can't see myself on TV, either. It just wouldn't be dignified. I'm sure you get that, even if nobody else does."

Nugget blew air through his nose, which didn't sound like support for Clint's position. Apparently even his horse was against him.

THE DAYS PASSED more quickly than Meg had expected. She wished the studio had come up with this bright idea in the summer, though, because she nearly froze to death in Colorado and Montana. In Montana they'd had to broadcast in the snow.

Although hitting cowboy-oriented states in alphabetical order meant more crisscross travel, the concept seemed to appeal to viewers. New Mexico was a little warmer, but not as balmy as Arizona. She remembered with longing the warm sunshine in Sonoita as she and Jamie headed to Oklahoma and then back down to Texas.

She thought of Clint with more than simple longing. Missing him desperately seemed to be what she did best these days. A thousand times she considered calling to find out if he'd had a change of heart, but she couldn't risk it. He might erase the tiny glow of hope that kept her going.

Her days were filled with watching cowboys perform, conducting interviews and broadcasting the results to a waiting audience that grew daily. The show's producers were ecstatic about the jump in ratings. Meg knew she should be ecstatic, too.

But she was too busy missing Clint to feel any satisfaction in the project's success. Even her worry that Mona would steal her spot had been bumped way down on her list of concerns. Instead, she had taken up a new hobby.

Most of the ranches had porches, and weather permitting, Meg had fallen into the habit of sitting on them in her spare time. None had quite the relaxing vista she'd found at the Circle W, but whenever she sat on a porch, she felt close to Clint.

She liked to imagine him sitting on his porch thinking of her at the same time she was thinking of him. The more she indulged this new hobby, the more she craved it. And the knot of anxiety about her career that had kept her in constant motion for the past several years began to disappear.

On the last afternoon of their odyssey, Meg sank onto a wooden chair on the porch of the Double D ranch in Greybull, Wyoming. From the porch she could see the Big Horn Mountains and she pretended they were the Santa Ritas that Clint saw from the front of his house.

She could use a cup of his industrial-strength coffee, because she was a little tired and had to be upbeat for the last finalist party tonight. After the broadcast in the morning, she and Jamie would return the live truck they'd rented in Cody and fly back to New York.

Jamie came out of the house with two mugs of coffee and sat down in the chair next to hers. "Not as strong as Clint's, but then, nothing is or ever will be." He handed her a steaming mug.

"Clint's coffee is now the gold standard for coffee strength." She didn't mention what else about the man had become her new criteria for excellence. It involved some private moments with Clint that Jamie still didn't know about.

"I talked to Alison just now."

Meg quickly turned to face him. "Really? Is this the first time since Arizona?"

"First time." Jamie sipped his coffee. "I promised myself I'd wait until we were headed home, and then make the call sound completely casual, like one friend to another."

"And?" Meg felt Jamie's excitement across the short distance between them.

"She dumped the other guy."

"Woo-hoo!" Meg leaped to her feet and went over to land a big smacker on Jamie's cheek. "That's awesome!

"I said that was interesting."

"Ah." Meg smiled and sat down again. "Playing it cool?"

"Sort of. I told her you and I were headed back tomorrow and I'd probably have tons of things to catch up on, so I'd call her when I got settled in."

"So you're going to call her like two minutes after you walk in your front door?"

"Probably." He grinned. "But I was proud of myself for not giving away the farm right away."

"I'm proud of you, too." She reached over and squeezed his shoulder, although she could barely feel him through the heavy coat he was wearing. She'd had to buy herself a ski jacket back in Colorado, and she wore it now for what might be her last porch-sitting episode in a long time.

He glanced over at her. "Glad to be going home?"

She turned and focused on the shadowy mountains on the horizon. "I hate to say this, but I've gotten used to this slower lifestyle. I'm wondering how I'll do once I'm back in Manhattan."

"You'll be acclimated in ten minutes."

"That's what I'm afraid of, that this peaceful feeling will disappear the minute I step off the plane at JFK."

"I've had enough peaceful feelings to last me a lifetime. It's been fun, but I get a buzz from all that big-city energy."

"I thought I did, too." She took another drink of her coffee. "Now I'm not so sure."

"Does Clint have anything to do with that?"

She turned to look at him. "Why would you think that?"

"Masculine intuition. Plus the fact that Tuck asked me if I thought there was any chemistry, and then I saw the way Clint was looking at you during that wild and crazy broadcast the last morning we were there. And you sniffled all the way to Phoenix, and if it was a cold like you said, it was the shortest cold in history."

Meg sighed. "Okay, there's something there, but it's hopeless."

"Nothing's ever hopeless, Megster."

"Some things are. He's refused to consider putting even his big toe into New York, and I might like more porch-sitting in my life, but I'm not ready to spend all my days on a ranch in the middle of nowhere so he won't ever have to leave his comfort zone."

"I'm glad you said that, because if that was the plan I'd have to take drastic measures. Kidnap you or something until you came to your senses. You'd go nuts being a full-time rancher's wife. Besides, it isn't even his ranch."

"But it should be." Frustration gripped her again. "And he could take a giant step toward getting it back if he wanted to."

"Which means it's out of your control."

"Uh-huh." She took a sip of coffee. "I hate when that happens."

CLINT WATCHED Meg's last broadcast, which was beamed from Wyoming. In fact, he'd watched every broadcast beginning with the one in Colorado right after she'd left the Circle W. He'd rearranged his entire weekday mornings so that he didn't miss *Meg and Mel*. Once the other guys found out, they'd joined him.

So that had become the routine—everyone gathered in the living room with a cup of coffee to catch a five-minute glimpse of Meg. Other than Clint, Denny paid the most attention, because in three days he'd be leaving for New York. Clint kept thinking about that during the last broadcast.

In three days, Denny would be on the set with Meg. He'd talk with Meg and reminisce about her days at the Circle W. She might ask about Clint and she might not. Clint didn't know how he'd stand it, knowing Denny was there and he wasn't, and wondering whether they talked about him at all.

Then after that he'd have to deal with Denny coming home again, having spent time with Meg. Another nightmare, as Denny would undoubtedly rave on about this and that in New York. Denny would know something about the city, about the studio. Clint would still be ignorant of all of it.

In the days following Meg's departure, Clint had spent his time taking greenhorns on trail rides and performing routine maintenance on the barn and corrals. He'd also confirmed with a vet that Gabriel needed rest before he could be put back in training. That dream was on hold indefinitely.

But in the late afternoons, Clint usually found himself on the porch drinking coffee and thinking about Meg. His conclusions made him uncomfortable, because he was beginning to realize that he cared more about Meg than he did about his dignity. He hadn't known he'd miss her this much, hadn't known the ache would be constant every waking minute. He had no idea how or if they could create a life together—he only knew they had to try.

She'd shown that she had the courage to come into his territory when she didn't know the first thing about it. She'd been willing to try anything, from his kick-ass coffee to sex in the shower. Then she'd battled her fear of horses in order to do the job she'd been hired for. Thinking of that, he felt like a yellow-bellied coward by comparison.

At the end of Meg's part of the show, Clint shut off the TV, as he always did. The boys didn't care about seeing Mel and Mona. They'd figured out that Mona had a mean streak and they could hardly wait for Meg to reclaim her co-host chair.

As the men started to leave for their various daily chores, Clint called them back. "I...uh, have something to discuss with you."

They each turned, and all of them looked nervous.

"George has a buyer, right?" Jed said. "I knew it had to happen some day."

"That's not it," Clint said. "Tuck knows about this, but maybe not the rest of you. When I accidentally ended up on TV that morning with the horses, I stirred up some interest with the people who run Meg's show."

"Oh, we all know about that," said Denny. "Tuck said not to mention it, though, 'cause it makes you real mad."

"Only because I'm an idiot," Clint said. Meg had told him he'd admit that some day. "Look, Denny, I don't want to steal your thunder, but I'm going with you. I've decided to be on that show, if they still want me."

Denny beamed. "Awesome! I don't stand a chance, but you do! The way we all see it, if you win, you'll get a bunch of money and maybe you can get the ranch back. Then our jobs will be safe."

Clint felt like the most selfish fool in the world. He'd been so caught up in preserving his precious dignity that he'd forgotten how an infusion of money could potentially protect his ranch hands. "I don't know if this will turn into a gold mine or not," he said, "but I've decided I'd be crazy not to go for it."

"That's great, boss." Jed came over to shake his hand, followed by José, Denny and finally, Tuck.

"You're doing the right thing," Tuck said, "for a bunch of reasons." He didn't say one of the reasons was Meg, but Clint knew that's what he meant.

"Are you gonna call Meg and tell her?" Denny asked.

Clint pictured doing that and rejected the idea. Advance warning would allow the studio to gear up for him and create more hullabaloo. He'd have enough trouble getting through this without giving them the chance to make it even more embarrassing.

"No," he said. "I think it'll be more dramatic if I just show up with Denny."

"It'll be dramatic, all right." Jed glanced at the ancient television set. "Wish we had something better to watch it on, though."

"Are you kidding?" José said. "We'll get the Steak Out to open up the bar for the show. Everybody will want to be together to watch it, anyway."

Jed smiled. "Great idea. So, boss, while you're on the show, remember, the whole town of Sonoita will be watching you!"

Clint's stomach began to churn. Exactly what he didn't want, but it wasn't as if he could stop them. Then he remembered Meg sitting bravely on Prince, white-knuckled and determined. He ignored his butterflies and smiled back at Jed. "I'll do my best to make you all proud."

MEG SAT in the makeup chair as Blythe finished with a dusting of translucent powder. The preshow makeup session seemed more tedious than it had been before she left. In fact, the parade of morning performances stretching into the future made Meg sigh.

Although Mona had tried to worm her way onto the show and cut Meg out, she hadn't succeeded. Her tactics had become so obvious that even Mel had commented on Mona's unbridled ambition. So Meg had the co-host spot sewed up. And she didn't want it anymore.

She didn't know what she wanted, exactly. Something in show business, but maybe not a daily TV show. She'd achieved her goal, and now she needed a new goal. Oh, and Clint. She still needed him as much or more than ever.

But she couldn't leave the show until the Hottest Cowboy in the West contest was wrapped up. She owed the contestants that much. They'd helped her pull the ratings up, and besides, they were good guys. Even Bill wasn't so bad, just immature.

By now they'd all be in the greenroom. She wanted to pay a quick visit there before show time, to say hello and make sure they were all happy with their hotel accommodations and the tours the studio had set up for them. They were a fun bunch. She could imagine them in there joking around as they waited for the big moment.

Blythe had unsnapped the makeup cape and Meg was about to get up when Sharon came barreling through the door, her cheeks pink with excitement. "He's *here!*"

Meg went blank. Was there a celebrity guest she'd forgotten about? The Hottest Cowboy thing was supposed to take up most of the show. They had booked a promising new country singer named Brad Daniels to tie in with the cowboy theme, but Sharon wouldn't get that worked up over him.

"Your cowboy!" Sharon said. "The one who held your horse and kept you from getting killed that day!"

Meg felt dizzy. "Clint?" But that couldn't be right. Clint wouldn't just show up. She squashed the sudden leap of joy she'd felt, because it was impossible to imagine Clint coming here unannounced. He didn't operate that way.

She cleared her throat. "You know, when you're not around them all the time, cowboys tend to look alike. I'll bet you're mixing him up with one of the other guys."

"No, I'm not!" Sharon looked as if she'd won the lottery. "We had seven states, three finalists each, so that's twenty-one cowboys. Number twenty-two is in the greenroom. And the audience will go crazy when they see him!"

Suddenly Meg had trouble breathing. Clint was really here? Apparently so. And if Sharon thought the audience would go crazy, she had no idea how crazy the co-host was going right this minute. She put a hand to her chest and forced air into her lungs.

"Meg?" Blythe leaned toward her. "Are you okay?"

"Yeah," Sharon said. "You look like you're having a heart attack or something."

Meg gulped for air, and finally the light-headedness subsided. She smiled at Blythe and Sharon. "I'm fine."

"Good." Sharon went back to her clipboard. "Here's what we'll do. We can't include him in the voting for Hottest Cowboy, because we have no time to explain him to the other contestants. But you and Mel can do a special interview with him later. We'll cut back on the band's time. Boy, I wonder if this guy realizes he's about to become a star."

Meg barely heard her. "If you'll excuse me, I think I'll pay a visit to the greenroom."

16

THE GREENROOM wasn't green. But it could have been purple for all Clint cared. He'd never been this scared in his life, not even when the Brahma bull had come bearing down on him. He'd rather face a herd of raging bulls than the cameras waiting for him out there.

Most of the cowboys were sitting on chairs or lounging on the two sofas at the far end of the room, but not Clint. He felt better standing near the door, so he wouldn't get surprised by anything. Besides, he didn't feel entirely welcome in that group. Except for Denny, they all wondered how he fit into the scheme of things, considering he hadn't been an official part of the contest.

Denny had stuck close to Clint, obviously giving moral support. "Relax, boss." He clapped him on the shoulder. "Nobody ever died from being on TV."

Clint glanced over at him. "You can't tell me you're not scared. When you're scared your freckles stand out, and I can see them real plain."

"You can? Maybe I should ask for some makeup."

Carlos got up from his chair and wandered over. "Nobody's putting makeup on *me*, that's for sure."

"I think Bill already put some on," Denny said.

Carlos snorted. "He would. Notice he's not hanging out with us. He knows better."

Although Clint still didn't have much respect for Bill, if it hadn't been for that worthless cowboy, Clint wouldn't be here. Sure, he was shaking in his boots, but he had a chance at making good money and working something out with Meg. She was somewhere in this building. The guys had all speculated on whether they'd see her before the show.

Clint didn't think so. He remembered how much time she needed to get ready, and she couldn't afford to run around checking on her guests and possibly make herself late. She was the star of the show, or at least the co-star. Clint understood that Mel was the main guy, but privately Clint thought Meg provided more sparkle. Then again, he was prejudiced.

"Did you know some of us already have fan clubs?" Carlos asked. "I just found that out from Hector over there, who heard it from one of the producers. After the show they'll give us the mail that's been coming in, and copies of the e-mails."

"Whoa." Denny blinked. "How embarrassing if you guys have a fan club and I don't."

"You can have mine," Clint said. "I don't want a—"

"Yes, you *do*," said Denny. "You want all that stuff, because you can turn it into cash." He rubbed his fingers together right under Clint's nose. "Don't forget why you're here, boss. You're gonna save the Circle W."

"Right." And try to save his relationship with Meg. He still wasn't sure what he'd say to her. He'd rehearsed several speeches, and none of them sounded right.

Carlos looked at his watch. "Shouldn't be long now. Any minute they'll—" He stopped speaking at the same moment every man in the room fell silent and those who were seated leaped to their feet.

Clint drew in a sharp breath. *Meg.* God, she looked beautiful. Much more beautiful than she did on TV, even more beautiful than he remembered from their time together. Her red hair shone in the light and her brown eyes sparkled. Her tailored green suit emphasized her incredible figure. Of course she had silly green shoes to match, shoes that showed off her pink toenail polish.

He wondered what the hell he'd been thinking, imagining that she'd want to work out a relationship with him. She was so gorgeous and famous that she could have anybody. Sure, he might have looked good to her when he was the only option available back in Sonoita, but she was miles out of reach now that she was back in New York.

Still, he was so glad to see her again, if only to say hello, if only to tell her that she'd been right and he was the biggest idiot the world had ever produced. The trip was worth it just for that. And he expected to get more for his effort, a chance to stockpile some money so eventually he could buy back the Circle W. By making that opportunity possible, she'd given him more than he deserved.

Her gaze swept the room and her amazing smile touched on everyone equally as she greeted each cowboy by name. Then she came to Clint. "What a surprise!" she said.

He wondered if he was the only one who noticed the slight quiver in her voice.

"I…uh, changed my mind." Boy, didn't he sound smooth.

"That's great! The audience is going to love this!"

The guy named Hector stepped forward. "You know, Meg, any one of us could have settled your horse for you. But we didn't get the chance."

"I know you could have, Hector. And that's why Clint

won't be part of the contest. One of the original twenty-one will be voted Hottest Cowboy."

Clint felt as if the air had been sucked out of his lungs. He wouldn't be able to compete? Had he made this trip for nothing? He glanced at Denny, who looked very upset.

Meg smiled at everyone again. Then she turned to Clint. "Could I see you out in the hall for a minute?"

Whistles and catcalls followed them out the door. She led the way down the hall and ducked into a small room that held a table, some chairs and a pop machine. A break room, most likely. This is where she'd read him the riot act about showing up unannounced. What a dumb idea that had been.

She grabbed his arm and gazed up at him. "I can't believe you came to New York!"

His cheeks burned. "I shouldn't have. I didn't realize I'd mess up the contest. I thought—"

"You're messing up nothing! But we can't let you be voted on, because we had no chance to prepare the other guys."

He felt like such a doofus. "You told me to let you know, but I didn't decide until the last minute. I wasn't thinking about how it would work with the other contestants." He'd only been thinking about seeing her again.

"Really, it's no big deal. The audience will eat you up with a spoon. You should see the bags of mail we've collected for you."

He stared at her, not understanding. "*Bags* of mail? You mean like the little plastic ones from the grocery store?"

"I mean like twenty-gallon trash bags. At least six. We have them in a storeroom, tagged. Some other guys have maybe one bag, if that. And the calls won't stop! Every caller, and they're mostly female, wants to know if we've booked you on the show yet. Quite a few asked if you're married."

Clint's brain went on overload. "Six twenty-gallon trash bags?"

"Yeah." She grinned. "Listen, I'm rushed for time, but I wanted you to know that Sharon, our executive producer, is already talking about bringing you back in a couple of weeks to find out all the ramifications for you. You're a celebrity." Her smile faltered. "Whether you want that or not."

He took a long, shaky breath. "I do want that. I mean, I don't, but I do. You were right. I need to earn what I can and try to buy back the ranch." He didn't have the courage to say more.

"Good. I'll help you through this, so don't worry. I'll set up a meeting with my agent if you want for later today."

"I guess…I guess I need one."

"Definitely. I'll see you after the show. And Clint…I'm so glad you decided to come." Then she stood on tiptoe, placed a quick kiss on his mouth, and hurried out of the room.

By some miracle Clint found his way back to the greenroom, which was a good thing because someone had arrived there to escort them onto the set. Clint walked along like a zombie as he tried to make sense of what Meg had told him. The good news was that money should start rolling in as a result of this. The bad news was that his old way of life might be gone, at least for a while.

Then there was the confusing part. Did Meg still want him, or not? He couldn't tell. She was happy that he'd decided to appear on the show, because it seemed like that would be good for ratings. High ratings would mean she'd keep the job that meant so much to her.

But he had no idea how she felt about a future relationship with him. After the show, he'd have to dredge up enough courage to ask her. Right now, he needed all the bravery he had for the ordeal ahead.

"What did she say?" Denny asked as they headed down a hallway.

"That it was okay for me to be on the show, and I'll probably need an agent." He didn't think mentioning the six twenty-gallon trash bags of mail would be tactful.

"So she thinks you'll get offers from this! That's awesome! I knew it was the right thing, you coming here."

"Guess so." He had to keep from passing out, though. That might tarnish his cowboy-hero image. Right now he was about fifty percent sure he could stay upright.

They arrived at a curtained-off area where several people ran around with headphones on and constantly put their fingers to their lips when they looked at the guys gathering there. From beyond the curtain came the sound of Meg and Mel giving their opening remarks interspersed with laughter and clapping from the studio audience.

Clint couldn't hear what they were saying because his ears were buzzing. Some young woman in jeans and a T-shirt came over with one of the microphone thingamajigs for him. She clipped part of it to the back of his belt and asked him to feed the tiny microphone up under his shirt and clip it on his collar. He was shaking so much he had trouble doing it, so Denny helped him.

Then another woman lined them up, with Clint last. One by one, she sent them through the curtain and out onto the stage. Clint had never parachuted from a plane, but he pictured it being like this—waiting your turn to leap and hoping you wouldn't freeze when your time came.

The crowd went crazy with each new cowboy introduced. Then they were down to three, then two, then one.

And it was Clint's turn. His stomach rolled, but he went through the curtain and plastered a smile on his face.

The audience was closer than he'd thought, and when he appeared, the noise was deafening. Women stood up and shouted his name. Others threw things onto the stage. Coins bounced and rolled on the floor, and a pair of women's panties sailed onto the set.

Mel got up, strolled to the edge of the stage and held up both hands. "Control yourselves, ladies! This poor man lives out in the middle of nowhere and doesn't see more than five people in a week! You're going to traumatize the guy! And by the way, how come you don't throw money and underwear at me when I come out?"

Amid much laughter and shouted comments, everyone sat down again.

"Okay, everyone!" Meg walked forward. "Now that you've had a peek at Clint Walker, I'm going to ask him to leave the stage. He's not an official Hottest Cowboy in the West contestant, but—"

She was interrupted by groans and shouts of dissent.

"But we'll bring him back for a special interview later! Don't worry—you'll be seeing a lot of Clint in the future!"

More cheers erupted, and a blonde who looked like a runway model came out to lead Clint back behind the curtain.

"I must have watched the tape of that thing you did with Meg's horse about a zillion times," she said in a low voice as they made their way offstage.

"It was really nothing special." Clint couldn't believe people were making such a big deal of that.

"Spoken like a true hero." She smiled at him. "Now stand right here, and someone will let you know when to go back out."

Clint nodded and took a deep breath. Well, he'd survived his first experience, and during the time he was out there he'd discovered two things. The longer he was on the set, the easier it was, and he was so fascinated watching Meg in action that he'd almost forgotten to be scared.

Any fool could tell she was a natural when it came to performing. She'd be involved in this kind of career for the rest of her life, whereas he'd be a temporary celebrity. No matter how he looked at it, he and Meg didn't have a very good chance of building a life together.

That depressed him so much that the buzzing in his ears let up and he was able to hear Meg interviewing each of the cowboys. Clint thought Denny did well, not sounding nervous or anything, but from the audience reaction, Hector had the contest won. Still, Denny would have something to tell his grandchildren.

Then Meg announced the voting and soon after Mel broke away for a commercial. A woman in headphones came over to Clint. "After the Hottest Cowboy is announced, and he's been congratulated and given his trophy and cash award, then all those guys will come off. You'll go back out and walk over to the living-room set on the far side of the stage. Sit in the chair on the right as you're facing the audience."

"Okay."

The woman smiled at him. "You're doing great."

"Thanks." He didn't think so. Compared to the relaxed way Meg behaved in front of the camera, he must look like a robot.

As the drum roll started for the announcement of the winner, he leaned forward, hoping against hope that Denny would get it. But Hector did, and the audience seemed really happy about it. Meg asked Hector what he planned to do with the money, and Hector said he'd buy a new pickup and a better horse.

Clint figured Hector would be able to buy more than that with the fame that would come his way, but maybe Hector hadn't thought that far ahead. Then Clint had no more time to think about Hector, because the guys were filing back through the curtain. Clint caught Denny's eye and gave him a thumbs-up.

Denny grinned back. Obviously, losing to Hector hadn't ruined his day.

"You're on," murmured the woman in the headphones, and gave Clint a gentle nudge.

His heart pounded as he returned to the set, but at least the feeling was slightly familiar, now. The audience clapped and cheered, but apparently they'd been warned not to throw things, because nothing came flying at him this time. As instructed, he walked over to where Meg and Mel stood next to a group of three chairs. He shook hands with Mel, but Meg gave him a kiss on the cheek, which everyone seemed to love.

"So tell us about this ranch in Arizona," Mel said as he settled into his chair.

"Uh…well, it's…beautiful." Clint heard himself and cringed inside.

"Yes, it is," Meg said. "And so peaceful. You should see the view from the porch, Mel. Clint, hasn't this ranch been in your family for generations?"

Then Clint understood what he was supposed to say. Focusing on Meg, he described the historic nature of the ranch. He talked about the changes that had taken place and even mentioned his dream of quarterhorse racing.

"Sounds idyllic," Mel said. "I know Meg can't talk

enough about what a great time she had there. I think you're hoping to pay another visit, right, Meg?"

"I would love to."

Clint wished he could tell if she meant that or not. "You're always welcome," he said.

"From the way she raved," Mel said, "I couldn't tell if it was the ranch or the rancher that had her so enthralled."

Clint had no idea how to respond to that. He glanced at Meg, whose smile seemed frozen in place.

"They go together." Meg met Clint's gaze. "I wouldn't be able to separate one from the other."

So maybe she had given up on him. But he couldn't leave New York without knowing for sure.

Mel waggled his eyebrows at Clint. "She's single, you know. Extremely single."

Meg's cheeks turned pink. "Why don't you put it in lights in Times Square?"

"I'm sure she's single because she wants to be," Clint said. "If she ever decides to get married, she could have her pick."

"My sentiments, exactly," Mel said. "But we're all getting impatient, waiting for her to do that!" Then he announced another commercial break.

Meg hurried over to Clint. "That was terrific."

"Thanks." Clint didn't think he had a snowball's chance in hell of seeing her again after today, but he'd decided not to leave without saying his piece. "Listen, can we have a minute to—"

"Yes. I've asked Julie, she's the blonde who escorted you offstage before, to take you back to my dressing room. Wait there. We'll get the musical part of the show out of the way, and then I'll be finished."

So he'd have some time alone with her. He'd have to make the most of it.

MEG COULD HAVE STRANGLED Mel for his broad matchmaking efforts. But it was done, now. As she hurried back to her dressing room after the show, she wondered if Clint was sitting in there thinking about whether this was some sort of marriage trap. She'd have to put his mind at ease right away.

After opening the door, she walked in and found Clint leaning against the wall of the tiny room. He looked too big, too masculine, and very uncomfortable. Of course he wouldn't want to use the girly chair in front of her dressing table, and that was the only place to sit. But she'd been so flustered by having him show up this morning that she hadn't been able to think straight about where to stash him until she could see him again.

"Listen, before we talk about anything else," she said, "I want you to know that I didn't put Mel up to those remarks this morning. I'm not trying to trap you into some long-term relationship. I—"

"You're not?" He pushed away from the wall and walked toward her. Two steps and he was within touching distance.

She looked into his eyes and their two weeks apart disappeared. Suddenly she was back at the Circle W, where they'd made love in front of the fire, in the shower, in his four-poster bed. At least she'd been making love. She couldn't speak for him. In his case, maybe it had only been sex.

With the kind of longing she felt right this minute, breathing became an afterthought. Mostly she wanted to kiss him. But she didn't know what he wanted. She decided to go for the light-hearted approach. "I'm not trying to hog-tie you, as they say out west."

He didn't smile. "I was sort of hoping you might be."

Now she really couldn't breathe very well. "You... were?"

"Yeah." His gaze grew tender. "I meant to lead up to this, but I might as well say it straight out. I seem to have fallen in love with you, and I—"

"You have?" Her heart beat frantically. This was far more than she'd dared hope for.

"I know it's ridiculous, with me being a cowboy in Arizona and you being a big star, but there it is. I can't seem to help myself. I've tried talking myself out of loving you, but it doesn't work."

Emotion tightened her throat, but she cleared it away because she had important things to say. "Please don't talk yourself out of it. Because I seem to be in love with you, too."

Joy flared in his eyes. "Really?"

She nodded.

"Do you want to be?"

"Yes. Yes, I do."

"That's a start." He reached for her.

She moved happily into his arms, back where she belonged. "We can build on it, don't you think?"

"Yeah. We can definitely build on it."

When he kissed her, he blotted out all the lonely days and nights she'd spent without him. She'd given up dreaming of his kiss, and now, miracle of miracles, his kisses were back.

Were they ever. In no time she started wondering if they could get it on right here on the floor. Probably a really bad idea. Someone would find out, and that wasn't how she wanted to end her career with this studio.

Clint seemed to have come to the same conclusion, because he released her and stepped back to gasp for breath.

"We should probably be a little careful. We have a tendency to get carried away."

"Right." Trembling, she fought for control when all she wanted was to rip those jeans right off him.

"And we have some details to work out."

"I know. But you're here! I thought everything was hopeless, but then you came to New York, so maybe it's not so hopeless."

Some of the joy left his expression. "But I can't live here all the time, Meg. What you said on the show is right. I don't want to leave the Circle W. My thought was to try and earn some money and find out if there was any chance for us, but I'm still an Arizona cowboy."

"I know, which is what I love about you. I wouldn't expect you to live here. That's what I meant when I said that on the show."

"But I'll visit," he said at once, relief in his voice. "I'll visit a lot. Tuck can handle the ranch so I can come to New York at least a couple of weekends a month. We'll make it work, I promise."

"How about this?" She caught both of his hands in hers, deeply moved. He was willing to sacrifice so much for her, and he wouldn't have to. "I'm ready to try Hollywood, Clint, but that doesn't mean I have to live there. Lots of Hollywood people live somewhere else."

"Like Arizona?"

"Uh-huh. That is, if you think you could stand to have me hanging around the ranch when I'm not working on a—"

"Good grief, woman." He pulled her into his arms again. "I want you to hang around, all right. Hang around constantly. Be there when I'm building a fire in the living room, when I'm taking a shower, when I'm so hot for you I'm ready to explode."

She wiggled against him. "Like now?"

"Exactly like now. You'd better figure out where we can go that has a bed in it. I'd suggest my hotel room, but I'm sharing with Denny."

"And I'd suggest my apartment, but this is the day they're treating our entire building for bugs, and we're not supposed to be there all day!"

"And I'll bet you have things to do." He cupped her bottom and held her tight against his erection.

"I do, and they all involve getting horizontal with you. Maybe we should just rent a hotel room."

"Good idea. We'll—"

A knock at the door made them jump apart.

"You guys still in there?" called Sharon.

Meg straightened her clothes and went to the door, but she only opened it a little way. "Hi, Sharon."

Sharon laughed, as if she knew exactly what had been going on a minute earlier. "I wanted to warn you that a bunch of reporters are outside, hoping to catch a glimpse of Mr. Killer Cowboy Charm, as we've suggested they call him."

"We should go out the back way, then."

Sharon's smile grew wider. "We?"

"Yes, *we*." It felt good to say it. "Can you get me the car service?"

"I can."

"And…and make it a limo…with tinted windows."

"Ooo, baby. You've got it." Sharon winked and closed the door.

"Thanks." Meg turned to Clint. "Well, now that you're a celebrity, you might as well start acting like one. We're going out the back exit, which is how we spirit away all the big stars."

"Did you just order a limo? Meg, I don't need a—"

"That's what you think. Ever made out in one?"

Slowly his look of concern became one of anticipation. "Nope."

She held out her hand. "Come on, cowboy. You showed me how it's done in the country. Now I'll show you how it's done in the big city."

He caught her hand and pulled her close again. "How dark are those tinted windows?"

She laughed. "Dark enough."

"This celebrity business may not be as bad as I thought. Okay, one for the road." He gave her a quick kiss. "Oh, and I have a request."

"Anything."

"Please don't ever call me Mr. Killer Cowboy Charm."

She smiled up at him. "How about husband? Would you answer to that?"

"Oh, yeah." His eyes glowed with happiness. "Definitely."

"Then I think we have a deal." As the two of them hurried out to the waiting limo, she anticipated the moment they'd be able to slow down and savor the next hour...the next week...the next year...a lifetime. There was no rush now. They had forever.

Epilogue

HERE THEY ARE, your *Mandy and Mel in the Morning* co-hosts, Mandy Franklin and Mel Harrison!

Meg stood backstage holding Clint's hand. What a surreal experience, to be here and yet not hosting the show. But it didn't bother her one bit. She gave Clint's hand a squeeze, and he leaned down.

"Miss it?" he murmured in her ear.

"Not even slightly." She spoke softly so that the mike attached to her lapel wouldn't pick up what she said. Earlier, she'd found out that Mona Swift had left television entirely and was running a PR firm. Meg felt no sense of triumph about that, either. She'd moved beyond petty jealousy.

Mel's voice drifted through the curtains. "We have two very special guests today, my former co-host, Meg Delancy, and Mr. Killer Cowboy Charm himself, Clint Walker! Evie and I attended their wedding out in Arizona several months ago, and let me tell you, Arizona is beautiful and *hot*. Nearly died of heat prostration during the ceremony."

Meg smiled. Their April wedding had been scheduled to take advantage of Arizona's springtime, but summer had arrived early. She and Clint had been married under sunny skies. *Very* sunny skies, with no shade for the guests. Mel had come back to New York with a sunburn.

As the intro continued, Meg listened to her replacement, instinctively critiquing her performance. She was excellent. Mandy set the perfect tone for working with Mel, sassy but never mouthy. She'd last a long time, if the current ratings were any indication.

Someone tapped Meg on the shoulder and she turned around to find Jamie right behind her. She pantomimed extreme joy and gave him a careful hug that didn't jiggle her mike.

Clint shook Jamie's hand and smiled. "How's Alison?" he asked quietly.

"Pregnant. Gorgeous." Jamie had put on a little weight, and he looked extremely satisfied and happy. He'd also been promoted, which was why he had the freedom to come over and talk with them.

Clint glanced at Meg, a question in his eyes.

She nodded. The news would be out in a few minutes, anyway.

"So's Meg," Clint said. Pride stuck out all over him.

Jamie's eyes widened as he turned to Meg. "Yeah?"

"Uh-huh." She still got the most ridiculous jolt of happiness every time she thought about their baby. People had kids all the time—no biggie. Maybe by the time she was six or seven months along she'd sing a different tune, but right now, at three months, she felt like doing commercials for motherhood.

Jamie gave her another hug and shook Clint's hand again. "That's fabulous. What's the due date?"

"Right about when the movie will be released," Meg said. "We'll probably be back then to plug it, if I can travel."

"If not, I'll talk Mel and Sharon into letting me come out and interview you at the Circle W."

"Come anytime," Clint said. "Don't leave it up to Mel and Sharon. Pack your bags and bring Alison."

"We'll try to do that. Listen, I have to get back to work, but we're looking forward to dinner tonight. Alison's in a cooking frenzy. She and José are shooting e-mails back and forth, exchanging recipes."

"One of these days, the two of them are going to make good on their plan to open a restaurant," Meg said.

"Yeah, if they can ever figure out whether to do it in New York or Arizona." Jamie turned to leave, still smiling. "See you two later."

"You guys are on," murmured a young woman wearing earphones.

Meg didn't recognize her and decided she must be new. Giving her a friendly smile of thanks, Meg took Clint's hand and walked onto the set. It hadn't been that long ago that she'd been in that woman's spot, yearning for a big break.

Mandy and Mel had moved to the living-room setup for the interview. After hugs and handshakes all around, Meg and Clint sat in two of the armchairs arranged in a semi-circle around a low coffee table.

"So the new movie's in the can," Mel said.

"Yes, it is." Meg appreciated the support Mel was giving her as she ventured into this new arena. She talked about the movie a little, mentioning her co-stars and the release date.

"Sounds like a great story," said Mandy, a brunette who looked like a young Sally Field.

Clint leaned forward in his chair. "It's terrific."

"Spoken like a proud hubby. And how about you, Mr. Killer Cowboy Charm?" Mel focused on Clint. "I understand that quarterhorse of yours, Gabriel, has done very well for you, so well that you bought that ranch right out from under my good friend George Forester."

Clint smiled. "We came to an agreement."

Meg was glad she'd get a tape of this show so that she could watch that smile again and again. Seeing Clint in possession of his beloved Circle W meant the world to her.

"Just as well it belongs to you," Mel said. "It's too hot for George, anyway. So tell me, is there a movie role out there tempting you off that ranch?"

"Nope." Clint glanced at Meg. "We have one actor in the family, and there she is. I've had my fill of the limelight."

"Well, we might have another actor in the family," Meg said. "You never know."

"I suppose you could be right." Clint started to glow again, the way he usually did when the baby was mentioned.

"Aha!" Mandy turned to Mel. "I think we just got some significant info."

Mel looked blank. "What info? That they might have another actor in the family? That could be anybody. Meg's brother-in-law, the one at the wedding who kept doing those impressions, or even her—"

Mandy put a hand on his arm. "I think Meg's trying to tell us that she and Clint are having a baby."

"You are?" Mel gazed at Meg, his eyes wide. "The Meg-ster's PG?"

Meg nodded.

"Why that's wonderful!" Mel leaped out of his seat to shake Clint's hand and give Meg a kiss on the cheek. "Congratulations! Wow, a movie and a baby." He sat down again and shook his head in obvious wonder. "Little did I know when you left for Arizona last year that you'd end up a Hollywood star, a rancher's wife and a mother, all in under twelve months. You move fast."

Meg reached over and took Clint's hand. "Actually, my new motto is to take it slow. Sit on the porch, watch the sunset, enjoy the peace and quiet."

Clint gazed fondly at her. "Exactly."

"I'm glad it works for you," Mel said. "Personally, I'd go stir-crazy out there in the middle of nowhere. All that time on your hands. Nothing to do."

Meg fought not to laugh. A year ago that would have been her opinion, too. But with a man like Clint around, nothing to do meant time for...other things.

"From the expression on her face, I think Meg enjoys that nothing to do part," Mandy said. "Let's not forget that she's living with Mr. Killer Cowboy Charm."

Mel glanced over at Meg and Clint and flushed. "Uh, well, yes! And this is a G-rated show, so we won't go there! In fact, we're out of time! Sharon's signaling that we desperately need a commercial break. But it's been super having you both on the show. Come back anytime."

Meg kept her laughter in check through the goodbyes, but when she and Clint were finally headed out the back exit toward a waiting limo, she started to chuckle. "Nothing to do," she said. "He walked right into that one, especially considering we'd just announced the baby."

Clint helped her into the limo. "Lots of time with nothing to do works for me. I was thinking maybe we could head back to the hotel, because I don't know about you, but I have all afternoon with nothing to do."

"Same here." She settled into the curve of his arm. "All those empty hours. How in the world can we fill them?"

He gazed at her. "Give me some time. Maybe I'll think of something."

"I'm counting on it." Then she pulled his head down for a long, lingering, limo-style kiss.

Silhouette Desire

MAN TALK

Silhouette Desire from *his* point of view.

BETWEEN DUTY AND DESIRE
by Leanne Banks
(Silhouette Desire #1599, on sale August 2004)

MEETING AT MIDNIGHT
by Eileen Wilks
(Silhouette Desire #1605, on sale September 2004)

LOST IN SENSATION
by Maureen Child
(Silhouette Desire #1611, on sale October 2004)

FOR SERVICES RENDERED
by Anne Marie Winston
(Silhouette Desire #1617, on sale November 2004)

Available at your favorite retail outlet.

Silhouette®
Desire®

introduces an exciting new family saga with

DYNASTIES : THE DANFORTHS

A family of prominence...
tested by scandal, sustained by passion!

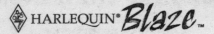
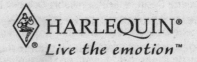